Praise for Spooky Lovers

"I want to say this loud and clear: *Spooky Lovers* needs to be on your TBR pile right now. Sweet, sad, and—true to its name—spooky, this novella is an absolute creepy delight from start to finish. I adored it, and if you love sapphic horror even half as much as I do, I bet you'll adore it too."

—Gwendolyn Kiste, Bram-Stoker©-Award-winning author of *Reluctant Immortals* and *The Haunting of Velkwood*

"JV Gachs summons a wickedly entertaining tale that's part Gothic love story, part murder mystery, and all spooky heart."

—Brian McAuley, USA-Today-bestselling author of *Breathe In, Bleed Out*

"*Spooky Lovers* is part murder mystery, part cozy love story, where the living and the dead intersect in a visceral dark comedy about finding peace and justice—dynamic, fast-paced, touching, yet haunting."

—Ai Jiang, Bram-Stoker©- and Nebula-Award-winning author of *Linghun*

"A mystery, a horror tale, or a phantasmagorical dream-like vision, a ghost story can be any one of these things, or all of them at once. With *Spooky Lovers*, J.V. Gachs demonstrates one more possible incarnation for the ghost story to take: a love story. Intriguing, breathtaking, awe-inspiring, and "awww"-inspiring, this novella's cross-genre appeal is found in Gachs's spookily effective execution and character work."

—Patrick Barb, author of *The Children's Horror* and *Pre-Approved for Haunting*

J.V. GACHS

MADAXEMEDIA.COM

Copyright © 2025 by J.V. Gachs

All rights reserved.

No part of this publication may be reproduced, distributed, or transmitted in any form or by any means, including photocopying, recording, or other electronic or mechanical methods, without the prior written permission of the publisher, except as permitted by U.S. copyright law. For permission requests, contact info@madaxemedia.com

The story, all names, characters, and incidents portrayed in this production are fictitious. No identification with actual persons (living or deceased), places, buildings, and products is intended or should be inferred.

Book Cover by J.V. Gachs

Interior Design by Joey Powell

Edited by Holly Lyn Walrath

Print ISBN: 978-1-966497-22-6

Ebook ISBN: 978-1-966497-23-3

CHAPTER 1

AVRA

To any sane person, meeting a stranger in an abandoned graveyard in the middle of the night would not seem like the best idea in the world. But most sane people don't visit graveyards for fun anyway, so what would they know? As someone who hosts a podcast about the most haunted graveyards in the world, I am more than happy to give this unusual first date a try. If a woman who suggests ghost hunting as a first date is not the love of my life, then I'm probably doomed to a lifetime of solitude.

Only the usual rain of Northern Spain accompanies me away from the city, up the hill, and down the old graveyard road. I've meant to visit this site for years, but somehow, the place managed to elude me, despite being only a couple of hours away from my hometown.

The graves here were exquisite statuary works of art in their time. It was the biggest cemetery in town until the church decided to move its location because of some ownership issues with the town hall. It was rumored that the new priest didn't like the size of his accommodations and pushed to be moved into a more luxurious home. Since then, it's become a ruin devoured by nature. The few living relatives of the graveyard's inhabitants took their loved ones' remains to the new cemetery, leaving their tombstones behind for lucky, spooky individuals like yours truly. Some forgotten souls, however, stayed in their original burial sites. No one asked for their lovely bones, and the town hall decided it would be too much trouble to relocate them when they were perfectly happy where they were. "Guarding the place," as some locals put it.

Once, my ex and I were going to have a date here, but then we had our biggest fight. She left the house the next day, and I never got to see this place.

This time, it's finally happening. The bus trip has been exciting. It's offered me the opportunity to read everything about the people still resting there, as well as the ghost stories surrounding the place, in the many articles I've collected over the years. I printed and bound them because your girl likes adding notes with a pen in between the lines, and you can't do that on your phone. There have been many ghost sightings at this place, some more believable than others. Unfortunately, people like inventing stories to make themselves feel important, and they don't realize the damage they've done to the credibility of *our* cause. The assholes.

The most repeated tale among those who've ventured into its gates is that of a lonely woman picking flowers, tending to the tombs, and feeding ravens. Translucid. Flickering like an old VHS movie. Pale and with all the markings that would make it clear to anyone with a pair of eyes that it was a spirit and not a regular woman. She's described as a friendly presence overall, but still scary nonetheless. Who wouldn't run home to their mothers after seeing a ghost, though? Even if said spirit was more preoccupied with gardening than with acknowledging the presence of human beings in her domain?

After first reading about the Marigold Girl, resisting the urge to go straight to the graveyard took all my might. But I promised Ernestina I would wait until midnight so we could unravel the mysteries together. Did I contemplate the possibility of doing it all the same and then lying about not having done so?

SPOOKY LOVERS

Yes.

But.

I do believe this woman is the love of my life, and that's not how I want our relationship to start.

The streetlamps cast a faint orange light over the road, projecting my shadow up and back as I walk. I take a video so I can add it to my vlog. An unkindness of ravens follows me, flying from lamppost to lamppost.

"What are you? The tour guides?" I ask them, smiling.

I met Ernestina on Spooky Lovers, "a neo-reality dating app for lovers of the occult, the macabre, and all things dark." While I'm not opposed to the idea of ending my days in the middle of the woods, living my best witchy life alone with a dozen friendly cats and a big dumb dog, I still wanted to give my cottagecore fantasies of companionship a try.

Originally developed for the training of elite military forces, neo-reality environments have become the latest craze in video games—and dating apps, apparently. They provide a first-person experience barely distinguishable from reality. All your senses are tricked into believing you are somewhere else. Touching, smelling, feeling. Tasting even. It is truly amazing what that technology can accomplish with only a pair of glasses, stickers, and gloves. I don't think I need to explain how it revolutionized the porn industry, right? However, what really made the new technology stand out was that it provided the means to be whomever you desired, to apply as many filters to your appearance as you pleased, to look however the hell you wanted. That's premium catfishing right there, with the seal of approval of all the app's one million users worldwide.

We clicked immediately. When I first met Ernestina, my virtual skin was dressed head to toe in black, with military boots and a shaved head. I gifted myself the latest expansion, with the muscular build my real-life, plump figure never allowed me to achieve. Sharp fangs. Clear skin. A straight nose. It was an extravagance, yes; but let's be serious, how could I resist?

Ernestina's virtual skin was that of a watery-eyed zombie with a red pinup dress and pink hair. The app was called Spooky Lovers for a reason. Since our first conversation, I've already crossed off sixty-three days on my calendar, and we've met in the neo-reality environment every single time. Considering our mutual interest in ghosts and the afterlife, this particular graveyard was the most romantic choice of locale for our first real-life date. Much better than a posh coffee place or a restaurant where I would have to pretend not to be the kind of woman who would eat a whole pizza in three bites and still have room for dessert.

I'm trying *so hard* to ignore the possibility that Ernestina is a catfish named Ernesto with a killer nickname like the Undertaker. One can't be sure with these neo-reality apps anymore. The filters are so good that my date could be a man with a mustache and thirsty eyes, and I wouldn't have a clue. This fear is more of a concern to my friends if I am honest with myself... The only possible outcome for this first date is love at first sight, moving in together, and adopting several pets. And not long after—summer would be okay—a discreet wedding in this same graveyard, wearing matching Victorian dresses—black, obviously—and having our recently adopted cats carry the rings on cute velvet cushions.

I stop walking and take my phone out of my backpack. Its front camera serves as a mirror.

Sigh.

Seeing my face partly covered by a reddish heart-shaped birthmark and my straight hair marred by successive pastel dyes, I'm considering turning back. The urge to run back home and cry myself to sleep is all too real. As real as the cawing of the ravens flying above me.

What?

Strong, independent women aren't allowed to have insecurities?

As weird as it might sound, we've never exchanged real photographs. Not one image that wasn't tainted by the app filters, anyway. Ernestina has been very insistent on the matter. I have suggested switching from Spooky Lovers to regular video calls or even meeting in person several times. I have the money and the time for the bus ride, after all. I only wanted to verify that this is a real connection. I've had previous bad experiences, investing time and feelings in people who were only looking to feed their own egos. The ones that pushed me closer to a single witchy future.

Ernestina, on the other hand, preferred to keep "the suspense," even after the first "I think I'm falling for you." She's stretched the rope as much as possible, making me almost lose my patience. Two nights ago, Ernestina finally gave in and suggested the graveyard date, knowing how I ached to visit it. I knew she wasn't all that comfortable with it, but I took the chance anyway before a changed mind could steal this special night from me.

I'm overwhelmed by eagerness and fear, but I've reached the rusty gates of the graveyard. They haven't been opened regularly in many years. Someone placed a chain on them to keep away anyone trying to sneak in, but that chain gave up on its job long before tonight.

I pause for a few seconds before lifting my chin, convincing myself I'm a person capable of facing any challenge fate might throw at me, except perhaps Ernesto the Undertaker. I place my keys in my fist like the claws of a wild animal, in case this is all a trap. No biggie. Just a precaution.

As one would expect, the gates creak as I open them. The ravens fly in as if they've been waiting for me to lead the way. The place is stunning. I try to imagine how it would've looked when it was still in use, and I'm convinced it's way more beautiful now. Moss-covered tombstones. Fungi climbing up the statues. Poison ivy reclaiming the weeping angels and mausoleums. The tones of the night are dark gray, black, and green. A path of fresh orange marigolds contrasts with the rest, as if they bloomed right then to welcome me. I kneel and pick one of the bright buds. It smells so sweet and fresh; all my fears dissipate. It convinces me that Ernestina and I will be lucky enough to encounter the Marigold Girl. Wouldn't that be an awesome story to tell our grandkids?

The first time we kissed, we saw a ghost.

Absolute perfection right there. I hide the keys in my pocket.

"A leap of faith, come on," I whisper to myself, wondering which one of us will carry our first child.

There's music in the distance. Nocturnal animals, unaccustomed to the presence of humans, watch me from the darkness, more surprised than scared. At the end of the road, a small, illuminated church waits. It's old and crooked, straight out of my spooky fantasies.

Against the light of the door, a figure's almost silhouetted. It carries a bouquet that seems to glow with a light of its own. *Wait, the figure seems to glow, too?*

"God, you're beautiful . . ." Although I still can't see the face hidden in the darkness, that sweet voice and the tone of delicious surprise in my date's voice warm my heart, dispelling all my doubts, if I ever had any.

I move forward, smiling. There stands the spitting image of Ernestina's neo-reality skin, gray-toned, with bloody, watery eyes included, only she looks like an old TV show, flickery and all. That's a cool effect. I wonder how she's doing it . . . I search for the lighting equipment. This woman is a box of Halloween goodies. She wears a black chiffon dress with embroidered constellations, though it's torn and ragged. Her hair falls over her shoulders. It's not pink but dark blonde, two thin bleached locks falling over her face. Tiny stars adorn her hair. Bruises all over her neck. Black and intense. Almost too real.

"Surprise?" She offers me the flowers.

I hesitate. It would've never occurred to me that Ernestina would be so brutally honest with her avatar. No one else is. After all, neo-reality environments allow you to pick and choose every little detail of your virtual appearance, and yet she decided not to change anything. Talk about self-confidence.

"Wicked makeup and such an amazing set of light effects—I'm so totally impressed," I laugh, biting my lip. "I don't look so much like . . . Well, nothing like my skin." There it is, a pang of shame.

"Well, it's not makeup, and there are no special effects either," my date replies, rubbing her cheek with a half-sideways smile.

I move closer.

Looking Ernestina up and down, I determine that there's no way the bloody, whitish gleam in her eyes could be fake. Not to mention the fact that I can fucking see through her? As someone whose favorite holiday is Halloween, I'm more than familiar with contacts and heavy, well-done makeup.

This . . . this is the goddamned real deal. Plus, she radiates cold and smells of jasmine.

"I hope you don't mind the chill," Ernestina smiles.

"You are . . . Are you . . . ?"

"Dead?" she helps. "Biologically, you could say so. It's up for debate what the definition of *alive* is, but in a broad sense . . . Yes. I am dead. After all, my heart stopped beating a long time ago . . . And I guess my body rotted and was eaten by a bunch of maggots and all kinds of bugs. But, anyway, here I am, right? A smell-of-flowers ghost. Maybe they'll canonize me one of these days. Ernestina, patron saint of the hot chicks. We can talk about it over dinner if you like."

As much as I'm terrified by the realization that I'm *actually* in front of a ghost, a very undeniably real ghost, I'm also smitten.

"As long as I'm not the dinner . . ." I reply, letting flirty-me take the wheel.

"Where've you read about flesh-eating ghosts? Aren't those zombies or vampires? How would I eat you, silly? Don't worry, I've ordered some delivery from the Japanese restaurant you mentioned."

I've got many examples of flesh-eating ghosts, but this is not the time to be Ms. Smarty Pants.

"How can you . . . ? Let's say I believe you are a ghost; how can you use a dating app or order food? How does that . . . this make any sense?"

"Well, see, some people came ghost hunting, and when they encountered a real ghost"—she points to herself—"they dropped that."

A phone half-hidden in the grass reflects the moonlight.

"Could you be nice and pick it up for me and put it somewhere safer, like inside the church? I always fear someone will take it away from me."

I take the phone from the ground, looking at her, confused. She rolls her eyes very dramatically as if she's read my mind.

"Oh, sweet Jesus, look."

She touches the phone with her translucid skin, and it lights up. She winks at me, and my phone vibrates.

"Get it," she says.

There's a message from her on Spooky Lovers. A winking emoji.

"How do you do it?"

"I don't know, I just do," she shrugs. "Zeros and ones dancing around me and . . . making sense."

Ernestina's voice is soft, not menacing at all. If she can be accused of anything, it's an excess of sincerity regarding her looks. This whole situation should be scary. I should be questioning my sanity, but the truth is Ernestina is right here in front of me, dead and talking, offering me flowers, and petting the ravens that accompanied me down the road.

Texting me with her fucking mind?

Is it legal to marry a ghost?

I enter the church without a second thought, put down my backpack, take off my jacket, and open the wine bottle I brought.

"How does it work? Do you have unfinished business? Is it some kind of curse or . . . ?"

"They didn't give me a manual the day I woke up under a ton of dirt, you know? I was lucky I managed to creep out."

"There's got to be some explanation for this, some purpose . . ."

"Why are *you* here? What is the purpose of your existence?" Ernestina sounds a bit annoyed.

I stare at my wine glass in silence. A lifetime spent enjoying all things dark only to question a real ghost when I encounter one. Shame on me.

"That's what I thought," Ernestina says, guessing my thoughts. ". . . I hope you won't change your mind about us now that you know I'm the ghost we were supposed to hunt down," Ernestina says.

I look up. Her eyes are full of doubt, of the same anguish that I felt approaching the graveyard. Tenderness floods me, and I realize that she's only lied to me because she had no other choice. What was she going to say? *By the way, I'm a ghost?* I close my eyes to picture myself as my virtual skin before taking a step toward the dead girl who is looking at me with wide, pleading eyes.

"Can I touch you?"

"I don't think so . . . But I can try to plug you in . . ."

Ernestina places a finger on the phone and another one on my hand. A jolt runs through my spine, like leftover electricity, tingling the tips of my toes and fingers. It has a metallic taste.

I find myself *inside* Spooky Lovers. My cyber tongue reaches up, looking for my fangs. Right. We're in the cemetery, yet also online, without stupidly expensive gloves and stickers. Wow. How much money could I have saved if I had met her earlier?

I reach out to make sure I can touch her as we've done before on the app. I gently stroke Ernestina's icy cheek, run my hand down her neck slowly, and barely brush my fingertips over the bruises visible above the neckline of her constellation dress. My palm rests on my date's chest. Her heart is not beating. I never thought anything of that before we met on the app. It's like pressing your palm against one of the tombstones. Ernestina shudders, her muscles tense, and her icy breath hangs in the night air. I grab her hand and pull it to my face, where Ernestina's frozen fingers trace my lips. My stomach turns. We relish every single second of anticipation before kissing. Slowly. Tongues caressing timidly. Teeth biting lips. Ernestina's skin turns warm, rosy, her eyes green and clean, and her bluish lips red, as if she's stolen some of my warmth. Her dress is brand new, and the bruises on her neck are gone. We laugh in surprise before kissing again and losing ourselves to one another. I wonder how we look from the outside, a woman holding a phone and a ghost floating in front of her.

Well, I have found the Marigolds' Girl after all.

Rain breaks out again. Darkness falls around us. Our kiss turns sour, her taste coppery. She struggles to breathe and takes a step back, eyes open unnaturally wide.

We disconnect from Spooky Lovers as I let the phone fall from my hands.

Ernestina grasps at her neck as if she is fighting someone's efforts to strangle her. She claws the air, trying to scratch some invisible face. Bloodflowers bloom in her eyes as an invisible force shakes her. She levitates, as raised by an invisible person; she's trying to hit something or someone with her legs. She gasps for air, for her life, but both are being taken away from her. Her dress rips. Her hair moves as if she is underwater as her head shakes. I hear bones snapping.

Ernestina falls, while I can't even move to help her, and the ground beneath her opens wide. Rocks and lava cover the floor. A portal to hell. The earth trembles and shrieks, and I fall backward. The heat's almost unbearable.

Black fire devours her limp body before the portal closes again.

Okay.

I was definitely not ready for this.

CHAPTER II

ERNESTINA

Oh, sweet Jesus, that was embarrassing.

For once, it's been something *other* than horrible and painful. I was so worried about ruining my date that I didn't focus on my neck snapping, or the pain in my wrist and between my thighs. The black fires from the pits of hell scorching my skin are nothing compared to the look in Avra's eyes. Those huge, beautiful, longing eyes were absolutely terrified for me . . .

Anyway, I'll take this knot in my stomach any day. It's a nice change from the usual endless despair and dread.

What a pity.

It was going so smoothly . . . She took it well, I think. Better than what I'd anticipated. I was ready to get my heart broken. And she's so pretty. I hadn't imagined her like that. Did I expect her to have sharp vampire fangs? Obviously not. But other than that . . . I don't know if I'd tried to picture her real self before. As soon as I saw her walking toward me, I was completely smitten.

That kiss. Well, that kiss was completely, absolutely, unquestionably mind-blowing.

While it lasted, my body came to . . . life.

Always the perfect timing, Ernestina. Always the perfect timing.

I wonder if Avra's still in the church waiting for me to recover from my . . . incident. It's more likely she's gone running up the hill back home, and I will never hear from her again. I wouldn't blame her. This is the ghost equivalent of puking all over her shoes right after our first kiss.

What would ghost vomit look like?

As usual, I'm back where I started, under a ton of dirt. I can't feel it, but the darkness is telling. There's a certain kind of deep-black, dense, muddy dark that can't be mistaken for a moonless night or having your eyes shut. It's the hopeless void of death, my forever resting place. If this wandering around, reliving the night my life ended, can be called *resting*.

I crawl out of the earth theatrically. Not that I need to, considering I don't have a body. I wish I were a zombie, I would be way scarier that way. I still find it amusing, the theatrics of an undead escaping hell to torture mortals, and it always puts me in a good mood to think some living soul might stumble upon the scene: a ghost in a beautiful gown, emerging from hell to haunt them. The screams. The running around aimlessly.

It's so invigorating. And I need to lighten up my mood after that catastrophic after-kiss.

Arrgh, beware the dead woman!

I cling to Ernestina's tombstone. I take a peek around.

No one.

Pity.

I revert to my regular nonmenacing self as soon as I realize there's no audience to perform for. There's a weeping angel above the tomb, hiding its face in its hands. Whoever paid for it really loved the woman buried here. It's not one of those mass-produced pieces. Actual human hands worked on it. It's ivory and . . .

gold? Something golden, anyway. A chryselephantine statue. Something my old self was familiar with, and a piece of knowledge worth keeping in the afterlife, apparently. Did I work in a museum? Was I an art teacher? A classicist? The attention to detail is next level. I've always doubted it's my weeping angel, my tombstone, or even my name. Shouldn't I be inside a coffin if it were? A soft, silky one instead of being buried in the dirt?

Ernestina had a nice ring to it—it sounded like the name of a poet, a crushed soul—so I adopted it after realizing I wasn't going to remember mine despite how hard I tried. I used to take long walks around the graveyard, reading the names on the stones out loud in case one tasted familiar on my fleshless tongue. I still do from time to time, even if I know damn well it won't make any difference. I enjoy it, inventing lives that could've been mine, had I been named Rebecca or Laura.

It's still dark outside. I have no way of knowing if it's the same night. It might as well be a month from yesterday. Sometimes I snap out of it a minute after; sometimes it takes a whole fucking year. I hope that's not the case this time. Avra would be pissed if I ghosted her like that.

Ha.

I float gently to the church, sprouting marigolds as I pass between the gravestones.

Languid and moaning. Being the designated ghost of an abandoned graveyard is a lot of work. And I love it. I gave myself the job after all, on the day I woke up under the weeping angel. My unkindness of ravens is happy to see me. They caw and fly around me, caressing my cheeks with their black feathers. My sweet creatures of the night. It's weird how I can touch these little shadows and the flowers I create, but nothing else. Not that I'm complaining. It would be unbearable otherwise, to be confined in my own mind, walking around the realm of the living, unable to participate in any way. Whoever decided it was a good idea to include ghosts in the design of this world was a psycho. How does it make any sense to add more suffering to your allotted pile?

Avra's not here. The phone is on the altar, hidden under a bunch of dried leaves, just as I asked her. So thoughtful of her after witnessing my murder . . . I tap on it.

It's been three days.

Fuck.

I look around, thinking about what I should do. Could I use the phone to call her? I've never tried that before, but it should work just as well. I'll need to figure out her number first. Do the Yellow Pages still exist? Oh, wait, there's a note under some dried-up flowers on the church's one remaining bench.

"I figure this is some kind of ghost-reliving-her-death thing? Can't say you didn't scare the hell out of me . . . But, hey, call or text when you come back. Loved that kiss xxoo."

Oh, my clever Avra. This is why you look for a companion on dating apps for lovers of the occult if you're a ghost. The users there get it. She gets me. Appreciates my weirdness. My twisted sense of humor. My odd looks. That's not the usual response I get. Or used to get, when I was alive. Maybe I was insufferable. But, really, can death have changed me so much? I don't think so. But I can't get rid of those high school bullies I barely remember, even though the only thing remaining of them is this nagging feeling that they did exist, and they hurt me.

They were real.

Just as I was flesh and bones once.

Sometimes I wonder how I can be so sure about these things from my past life. About anything, really. It's weird how the brain works in the afterlife. Why it keeps some bits of information and not others to accompany you for the rest of eternity. Why some memories are faded feelings one can't really name, like a word on the tip of your tongue, eluding you. While others are clear as full-moon nights.

I know I liked huevos rotos con jamón. I don't necessarily remember how it actually tastes. But I know I liked it. How is that useful for anything? My

SPOOKY LOVERS

favorite song was "The Man Who Sold the World," but despite my efforts and my access to the internet, anytime I want to play it, it just sounds like pink noise, and I forget why I was looking for it in the first place. I hated getting up early. There's an irritating numbness I get sometimes that bothers me a lot because nothing can be done about it. Eventually, it just disappears, same as it shows up: unannounced and unpredictable. I can't remember what sleeping felt like, but I believe it must have been something similar to that tiredness. My limbs get heavy and my vision blurs. Sometimes it precedes the reliving of my death, but not always.

For me, the worst thing about this selective forgetfulness is how my name eludes me. Do . . . Did I have a family? Friends? Where was I going in this beautiful gown? It must have been a party, right? Did I have a date? Is someone still waiting for me with a bouquet and butterflies in their stomach? Have tears been shed for my death? Is someone looking for me? If only I could remember anything useful from the time I was alive, maybe I could stop this anxious feeling, this reliving-my-death bullshit. Maybe I could be free. Go into the light or whatever.

But I wouldn't have a chance to spend more time with Avra then . . . and we have so many things to do together. So many years ahead of us. Eternity, in my case. Maybe also in hers if we manage to fabricate some unfinished business for her before she passes, hopefully at a hundred years old, happy in her bed, unharmed. I love that woman. Deep in my heart, I wish we'd met before I died.

Anyway.

There's no point in dwelling on these hypothetical situations. I'll never get the chance to know who I was. There's only who I am now, a ghost woman hopelessly in love with a living one.

Logging into Spooky Lovers.

Open chat.

Avra, u there?

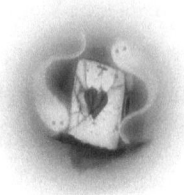

I draw a passage of bright flowers for Avra, to surprise her and welcome her back. Tonight they are purple, though, because I'm afraid of seeing her.

Breathe in, breathe out. Everything is going to be okay.

The marigolds turn orange as my nerves calm.

That's better.

My sweet, alive girl agreed to meet me again. I've planned the perfect date to the best of my ghost abilities, which are quite a few when you have unlimited access to the internet, and you don't really have to pay for stuff . . . *Wink*. We're having—*she's* having her favorite Italian dish, Fiori di Zucca, Lambrusco, and chocolate cake for dessert. I've created a playlist and managed to get a ton of candles to light the church up. I also bought some cozy blankets and a futon so she can be comfortable after it gets dark and cold. I would love for her to spend the night with me.

Avra wasn't angry or even confused when we talked on the app. Most people would be at least a bit resistant. Worried it would happen again? She was very understanding about the whole "Hey, I'm a ghost, by the way. I do reenact my death from time to time" thing . . .

Maybe too much?

"What do you think, friends?" I ask my ravens. "Does she like me? For real? Yay or nay?" They caw and fly in circles around me. "Did you like her? You better, because she's going to be around here a lot. I hope she feels the same way about me, about who I am now, and not just because she thinks she can get evidence of a real ghost for her stupid podcast."

The flowers turn bright red, and my ravens fly away scared. Wind rises. Thunder explodes in the distance, or maybe it's just inside my head. It's difficult to know what happens inside my little kingdom of dead things and what is also transcending to the realm of the living.

"I'm not going to give her an interview or anything like that. *Prfffs*. Who does she think she is? Scully? If that's what she wants, to broadcast my existence to the world, she can forget about it and fuck off all the way to the moon. If she ever asks about filming me or taking my picture, I swear I'll haunt her whole family. For generations. The audacity. She better look for another spirit. I'm not a freak, not a circus attraction. Is the only thing interesting about me that I'm a ghost? I might not remember who I was, but I am someone now. I am more than my death, damn it. Fuck her ghost-hunting ass."

The flowers turn black as my mood sinks into a desperation pit. Heavy rain seeps into my dead bones. I'm ice cold.

"Hey, Ghosty, you okay?"

I turn around to meet Avra's raised brows. She's leaning against one of the tombstones. The rain stops, and the world around me reveals itself. It's a warm, moonless night. No thunder, no rain. My flowers close over themselves, mimicking my embarrassment. If only I could just puff in the air like the ghosts in movies . . .

"Humm . . . Oh. Hi . . . How long have you been there?"

"Long enough, I'm afraid," she chuckles. "Let me tell you, that's all bullshit. You are just afraid, and I get it. I'm afraid, too. This feeling gets to you, doesn't it? But, hey . . ."

She comes closer. "I don't like you because you are dead. I hope it goes without saying that I would very much love for you to be alive so I could kiss you right now. Also, just so you know, I don't like you because you have the most knowledge of 80s horror movies or whatever lies you've told yourself about why I like you this much. Do you really think I wouldn't realize you were searching online for those things? I thought it was cute you wanted to impress me and made a list of movies we had to watch together. See?"

She lifts her phone in the air for me to see a "Movies Ernestina Pretended To Like <3" list.

"So, I'm not even good at pretending..."

"No, no, nena. What I'm trying to say is... that I like your sense of humor. All those ghost jokes have a whole different meaning now, and they're hilarious. I like the nicknames you give me. I like your voice and the way you talk, the way you move, and how you make me feel special and cared for. The fact that you did not hide your appearance as the rest of us do, how you always remember everything I tell you, and the excitement in your voice when you talk about gardening and birds."

"How can you like me when I don't know if I like myself? Ernestina isn't even my real name. I don't remember who I was when I was alive. I don't know anything about the woman I was. I'm just an eggshell. I'm empty."

I can't help crying. Avra reaches out to hug me, but I turn to golden dust in her embrace, a warm tickling feeling, and only become whole again when she takes a step back.

"Oh, Ghosty... I could help you with that. I'm good at investigating. I am so, so sure we both would love the woman you used to be. Do you want to remember so we can share our awful first-time experiences? Learn what movies you did like for real? Complain about how high school was awful and about our first jobs?" Avra asks with a tender voice that makes me laugh.

"I do."

CHAPTER III

AVRA

I smile like an idiot while purchasing the bus tickets, despite my lack of sleep and caffeine. Then, while I wait for the station machine to deliver my hideous coffee, I remember my promise to help Ernestina find out who she was and what happened to her.

My heart sinks.

Where to begin? Some online page for missing people? She has tried that already, I'm sure. The cops? Maybe the library? A newspaper?

Fuck.

I might have overestimated my ability to help Ernestina, and now I'm going to be another disappointment in her afterlife. I hated watching her so upset. What else could I have said? If she feels lost, and finding out who she was would change that, how could I not offer to help her? It crushed my heart to see her relive her death, gasping for air, fighting like an animal to set herself free. Powerless. How many times has she gone through that torture? Wasn't it enough to be killed once? Maybe if we manage to find out what happened, she can stop it from happening again, like that movie with Liam Neeson and Daryl Hannah... What was it called? It will come to me... You know, the one with the ghosts. *High Spirits*!

Ernestina hasn't disclosed the details of what happened the night of her murder, whatever it is she remembers anyway, but what I saw the other night was very self-explanatory... If we could stop it from happening again, then we could sort out the particulars of how to make a relationship work between my pulsing heart and her still one. The matching Victorian wedding dresses are obviously out of the question, but we have the app to allow us to be physical and to contact each other. It really isn't that different from a long-distance relationship. Only better. Plus, the newly discovered tickling game. I've never felt anything so powerful in my life. It left us both exhausted, and it's so rare that it's probably better to save it for special occasions. You don't want to turn that into a mundane feeling.

In the heat of the moment, claiming, no, promising I would help her and solve all her troubles struck me as the most romantic thing I could do for her. In the three seconds it took me to respond, all the different scenarios of me revealing her past crossed my mind. The tears. The hugs. The sweet cyber-lovemaking. Unfortunately, just the outcome of that last one came to mind, not the process. It shouldn't be so difficult, considering the tools we have nowadays. We have neo-reality environments, for fuck's sake... One only needs to focus and think hard on the resources at hand, and how to use them properly...

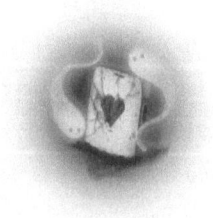

SPOOKY LOVERS

Spending the night with a ghost woman was quite different from any previous dating experience. At least this time, she didn't relive her death. That would've been way too much for a third date, even for me.

"Shall I . . . ?" Ernestina pointed at the phone once the tears had dried on her cheeks and on my sleeves. We'd sat inside the abandoned church for hours, talking about nothing, yet having the most meaningful conversation I've had in years. Then silence fell upon us. Eyes locked on one another. My heart raced. I wanted her so bad, but I ached for something more than an app to stimulate my nerves.

"Wait, could we try something first?"

"Sure," she answered with a curious look.

I sat cross-legged on the floor of the church, and she imitated me. Only, she did more than sit: She hovered over the gray, broken tiles. We were so close that her jasmine scent was intoxicating. I drew my hands forward, palms up.

"Hold my hands," I said.

"You know I can't do that. You saw what happened when you tried to hold me before. I just turn to smoke and speckles."

"I know, I know, but I felt something as you dissolved in my arms . . . some tickling. Didn't you? The worst thing that can happen if we try is that nothing happens. Come on, Ghosty. Let's try."

She sighed and rolled her eyes. But smiled, shaking her head.

"Okay. You won't always get your way, you know that?"

"Yes, I'm very aware, ma'am."

Ernestina chuckled and raised her hands. Hesitantly, she moved her palms closer to mine. The closer she got, the colder my hands turned. She stopped, mere millimeters from my skin. It was like touching a source of electricity. A humming sensation gave me shivers and tickled the back of my spine.

"Do you feel that?" I asked, laughing.

"Yes," she murmured.

Then, she placed her hands over mine, then in mine. It was a building sensation, quite similar to that of an approaching orgasm. My whole body vibrated. Warmed. It was tense. Strong.

"Fuck," I whimpered, retrieving my hands.

"Wow . . . that was . . . that was . . ."

"Amazing," I finished the sentence for her. "See, it worked. We are gonna have so much fun, Ghosty."

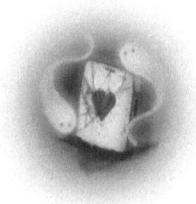

I fell asleep on the bus back despite the shot of caffeine from the station machine. Now, my brain has turned to mashed potatoes. I walk into the local radio station that allows me to record my podcast at a reasonable fee. I still have to record this week's show. Some half-cooked research I managed to do about Bloody Mary on the ride here before falling asleep like an idiot will have to do. It's not like there are masses of people waiting for me. No one will notice if I don't post the weekly episode, but I'd notice. I would know. And I would've failed myself.

The radio station is small, old, outdated, and it's now owned by a youth social club. They are very nice young people who play chess and learn crafts, and they also print a fanzine and broadcast some shows during the daytime. I used to come here when I was a teen, but now that I'm in my late twenties, I just use it for my podcast. It's an easy way for the club to make a few coins by renting the space to the gazillion people with podcasts in town. We could all record our little shows at home, but God, doesn't it look cool to do it here? And yes, it also sounds better, of course.

I'm lost in my own inability to know where to start my search when I bump into Andrea. She's just as stunning as ever. I get distracted for a second when she winks at me. Tease. She still has this effect on me whenever we cross paths, despite how hard I try not to be attracted to her pink lips or her soft skin . . . It never works out, and I know damned well why. Andrea's my ex-girlfriend and the host of *Gone for Good*, a missing-persons, true-crime pod . . .

Wait a minute.

"Andrea! Andrea, wait!"

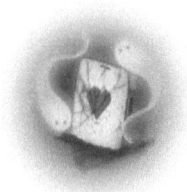

I can't stop thinking that I'm losing my spot for recording tonight, and how I will have to record my episode inside the wardrobe (again) while I wait for Andrea to reply, to tell me something, and to acknowledge in some way that she understands what I have just told her.

She's put some sugar in her coffee and is picking at the lost grains on the table with her finger. She's immersed in her own thoughts, as if she were alone. Was she even listening? Her fingers trace an elegant path from the table to her lips, to her tongue. Then, she notices me again. She stops, leans back in the chair, takes a sip, and finally speaks.

"So, tell me again why you want to know about this woman." Andrea dips her croissant in her café con leche. We are in our favorite café. They serve pastries throughout the day, so even if it's dinner time, we're having breakfast. I'm having toast with olive oil and tomato. Being here with her brings back so many memories. Having breakfast together here was our favorite—no, second favorite thing to do together when we first met. It's been more than ten years since that night. We've been lovers, friends, a couple, mortal enemies, acquaintances, friends again, lovers, a couple, lost souls . . . The cycle seemed like a never-ending story. After our last breakup, I was sure we'd be back together at some point. But we remained friends. And that's when I knew that we would never be. She cared for me, but not enough to hate me for not being able to be the woman she needed. Who I was was more than enough to be her friend, though. And we have been friends ever since. She's got another woman now. One who makes her truly happy, one who's good for her.

She only agreed to talk to me about my latest crazy idea if I treated her to one of her favorite delicious pastries. It's arguably logical. It's not the first time I've had lunatic ideas and dragged her into them. I hate to admit that my tendency to do so ranks very high on the list of reasons why our romantic relationships never worked out.

I'd only confess that to her face in the presence of a lawyer or under torture.

"Well, there's this . . . presence in the old graveyard, you know, the one we were going to visit on our anniversary when . . ."

Andrea looks at me defiantly, leaving the croissant on its plate and crossing her hands in *that* way.

Maybe it's not a good idea to remind her of our biggest fight if I want her help. "Never mind, you know the one. I've been researching the many accounts of encounters with this ghost. They're all too similar. Everyone who has seen her gives the same specific details, and I want to check if there might be some real thing behind it. Some crime that's been overlooked? Wouldn't it be cool if my podcast could help yours? I mean . . . teamwork. If there's nothing, we would have lost a couple of days together, catching up. And if maybe she's a woman that got lost or kidnapped or whatever, maybe we both get super-cool special episodes."

She raises her brows, disapproval all over her face.

"And help a family know what happened to their loved one, of course."

SPOOKY LOVERS

"I know you're not telling me something, and I really, *really* hope you are not trying to get me into any trouble with Eva again. She'd be pissed if she knew I was going to help you with one of your potentially dangerous ideas. Like the train one. She likes you, but you tend to . . . push too much."

"This is different and totally safe. Cross my heart and hope to die," I reply with my best good-girl eyes.

"Okay, as always, I'm intrigued by your mere craziness. Tell me, Loca, what do we know about this ghost woman?"

CHAPTER IV
ERNESTINA

I t always begins with the void.

Darkness falls over me, confining me in my own little world of shadows. Then, flickering golden lights start popping up around me. Candles. Or maybe a string of lightbulbs. There's distant music. Classical. It's a string quartet, I think. The tune's familiar, although I can never remember it clearly enough to even hum it once the scene is cut—fade to black.

My gown's brand-new. Black silk and dark-blue tulle. Golden specks and constellations. It smells of spring. I sprayed some of my mother's perfume on it, but I can't even picture her. I remember the small turquoise bottle with a diffuser. It looked like something right out of a 50s movie. The sweet, flowery smell surrounds me. The tulle of the dress is a bit itchy under my armpits. Even though it's my size, it's tight. I have something on my face. A black masque. Lace. I can't see it, but somehow, I'm sure it's so pretty that it brought tears of excitement to my eyes when I first tried it on. My sister made it for me. I hate those specific details, clear sensations that amount to a big pile of nothing useful. The masque matches the stars in my hair and the constellations on my dress. My lips taste of glossy strawberry lipstick. There are figures around me, eyes hidden behind other masques, beautiful dresses, tuxedos, black ties, gloved hands, and shiny shoes. My heart beats fast and my chest bursts with laughter. I've been waiting for this moment for ages, and I'm having the time of my life. I'm so nervous my stomach hurts. My cheeks turn red. I'm embarrassed and excited, aroused even. My hand, in lace gloves, rests in a man's hand. The music sounds closer now. I'm spinning. His other hand is on my back. It's warm. Too warm, as if he had a fever. We are dancing. He's wearing a black leather masque: a raven.

He has a beard. Gray. I want his lips. That longing is tainted by another feeling. I shouldn't want him. It's not right somehow, yet it feels so innocent, so tender. Young infatuation. I've loved other people. I've had relationships. The ache of those lost loves still lingers in my heart, but this is different. *He* is different.

My sex is wet, desire and butterflies in my chest.

But something changes abruptly. It doesn't feel right anymore. My stomach shrinks. I gag.

No.

I don't want this.

Stop.

My heart pounds in a different way. Fear. I'm terrified.

I need to go.

To escape.

I'm running, but my high heels are trapped in the mud. I throw them away. The earth is cold and damp under my bare feet. Still, I can't run very fast. The dress is heavy. It drags on the ground, getting stuck in the mud and twigs. Then, a familiar sharp pain crosses my wrist.

That's when my death sequence really starts.

An invisible hand grabbing me. Hard. It broke my wrist, but lucky for me, the afterlife is healing. I only ever feel any pain when I'm submerged in this state. After the pain, there's always chapped lips and a beard smearing my strawberry lipstick. The salty taste of tears. The soft stroke of the raven's feather on my neck making my back stiff. My feet don't touch the floor anymore. I can't breathe. I can't breathe. An explosion of pain between my thighs. I fight, hope pushing me forward, my gown torn as I fall to the ground. And a second later, I'm flying.

Then there's a push. Snapping sounds.

But this time, something's different.

Avra's spending the night with me again inside the church. She's on the futon with the comfy blankets I purchased for her. Going back and forth on the bus has her exhausted. Yesterday, she was so happy. She's got someone to help with my case. She calls it "my case," and I love how dedicated she is, but I'm not sure they'll be able to discover anything.

Obviously, I don't sleep, but I like watching her do it. She's peaceful, beautiful. And she snores, which I find terribly cute.

Then, darkness falls.

Oh, no, nonono.

Everything goes as usual, until, across time and space, ripping the veil between life and death, I hear Avra's screams while I float, grabbing at the invisible hand that's killing me. Her piercing howl allows me to focus, to be present, instead of vaguely there, hiding in the darkest corners of my brain to avoid the pain. Now, I look straight into his eyes. Gray eyes full of a twisted hunger behind a raven's masque. He wants to devour me, and air is the only thing keeping him from doing so. Where my own feelings were naïve and tender, his are sharp and twisted, like a crown of thorns. He knows exactly what he craves, and he is getting it. Wishing to escape my own suffering, I pour myself inside him.

I'm on the other side now.

He has big hands. Soft. He doesn't do manual labor. One of his hands is enough to trap my whole neck and squeeze the air out of me. He doesn't even need to use his whole strength. There's an immense urge inside him, here with me. It's infecting me as well. It's revolting. But there are also choices inside him, all around me, floating like afterthoughts of his decision to pursue his fantasies this evening. I try to press on that idea, to balance it out. He could stop if only he wanted to. But I'm inside a memory, an echo. Nothing I can do would change what happened to me. He decided. He could've stopped.

If only.

My heart breaks.

Through his gray eyes, I see myself, my pleading expression of betrayal and fear. I'm flesh and bones, pain and fight. It thrills him. His feelings revolt me because I'm still inside him after my body falls limply to the ground. I'm still inside him as he tears my underwear and unzips his trousers. I didn't need to know that. Those were not the dark flames of hell burning my skin, hurting me every time I relive this moment. The pyre I burned in was just his sick lust. I shut my eyes, try to hide from his nerves, from the pleasure he stole from me.

I want out.

I want out.

I.

Want.

Out.

He's done. I'm done. My body is nothing more than a broken porcelain doll beneath his. No one disturbs him. No one has seen. The moonless night and the woods protect him as he planned. The taste of strawberry lipstick lingers on his tongue.

My eyes are still open, reflecting the darkness of night.

He looks at me, hoping he can keep me like this forever. But when he touches my skin again, it's already turning cold. My smell is fading. He then takes a piece of my dress and smells it. My mom's perfume is sprayed on it. The flowers. Even that he's stolen from me. My last memory, he shares. He's got scissors in his pocket. He was prepared for this moment; he'd anticipated it for months, and it was just as good as he'd hoped. He cuts a lock of my hair and puts both items in a plastic bag. He carries me to a car. A black car. I wish I knew something about cars so I could tell Avra what model this is. I'm sure that'd help find him. Punish him. Stop him. My body on his shoulder is not heavy at all. I'm as light as a feather, getting stiff as a board. Then we're here, in the abandoned graveyard. The earth has been removed from many tombs already. Someone did half the job for him. He dumps me. My eyes are still open when the first shovelful of earth falls on my face.

And I fade...

I've crossed a line. As I fall back inside the darkness of my burial site, I cross other women. Faces as afraid as mine was. The same expressions of betrayal and disbelief.

Oh, no. There are more. More bones. More pain. More lost, nameless women.

From Ernestina's tomb, I can hear Avra still screaming inside the church. It was long for me, but by the looks of it, no more than a few seconds have passed for her this time.

"Hey, hey, I'm here, I'm back. It's okay." I try to calm her down.

"Oh, Dios, are you okay? It was different this time. You scared me for real," she replies. "You looked like . . . an animal. And you were mumbling things before disappearing."

"Was I? . . . It was all like it always is, but then I heard your scream, and suddenly I was able to get inside him or something. He has gray eyes and a big old black car . . . Is that helpful to find me?" I'm panicking now as I realize what it all truly means. "I was inside him, while he . . . he . . . he took something of me. And I'm not the only one. There are more. It was terrifying to be inside of him, but what if . . . what if he's still alive? His hunger, it's not going away. He won't stop; he likes it too much. I'm not the last one."

I consider what I've seen tonight, and then speak my fear: "I was the first."

CHAPTER V
AVRA

Saying goodbye to Ernestina this morning took all my might and then some more. But now, finding out who she is isn't just a matter of helping her stop reliving her death. Now, we could be putting a murderous bastard behind bars. From what she saw, her family might still be looking for her. There's a reason why she couldn't find her grave. She doesn't have a proper one. She's not just a dead body. She's a crime victim with unfinished business. She is a nameless woman, buried and discarded like trash. She is one of las Otras, as Andrea calls the missing women who vanish into thin air. Andrea says it's the biggest tribe on earth.

Andrea picks me up at the bus station in the car we bought together but that she kept after we broke up. My heart skips a beat when I sit next to her. There are too many memories inside this old red Volkswagen Polo: the trip to Paris, the fight over gas, the stain from the hamburger I had that she always complained about.

"So, where do we start our quest?" I ask, trying to suck the feeling up. There are way more important things to think about than wallowing in self-pity or grieving the life we didn't have.

"Where all the better quests begin, my dear companion . . . at the oldest library available."

We drive back to the town I've just left. I could've saved myself a trip, but I wasn't ready to tell her that I'd spent the night at the graveyard with the ghost of the woman whose murder we're now investigating. At least not yet.

The library is old and gothic. If I were to say what type of building it is from the outside, a public library wouldn't even be on my list. Villain's lair? Eccentric rich man's mansion? Sure thing. Hollywood set?

"I love coming here for research," Andrea explains. "Not only do they have a huge collection, but it's also such a beautiful place. And it's never busy. I'm afraid they'll want to close it soon. They tried in the 90s, but the community came together and saved it. See, they're having a ball this weekend to commemorate the seventy-fifth anniversary and twenty-fifth since it was saved."

Andrea's so excited about this research. I guess I would be, too, if I didn't know there were lives on the line. What if we can't find anything? What can be done then? Living without knowing who you were would be one thing for Ernestina, but knowing he's doing the same to other women without being able to do anything . . .

That would kill her.

Again.

SPOOKY LOVERS

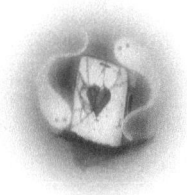

Andrea's the most efficient user of search engines and library resources I've ever known. That's probably why her podcast is so much more successful than mine. She's even managed to solve some cold cases and disappearances, helping the police out. That must be the greatest achievement for a show dedicated to missing people like hers. I seriously have no idea how she does it. I think having a community of dedicated sleuths helps, but I don't want to take away even a shred of her merit. *Gone for Good* is about to leave us indies behind and go mainstream. She's talking with someone at a real radio station, a proper one. And she's trying to sort out how to become part of their team, but she wants to keep creative control of her baby while they just want to profit from her well-deserved good reputation. One way or another, Andrea's going to be a big deal in no time. You'll see.

She gets out of the car, determined and full of energy. I follow her as the guard at the door greets her by name. She does come here often, by the looks of it.

"Another case, Andi?" The guard asks with a wink. "May I get a spoiler? I promise not to tell anyone."

"Yeah, like I would trust you again. You know me, las Otras are always calling me on duty, but you'll have to wait and listen to this one. It's special."

"Oh, jeez, specials are my favorites. Have a good time investigating, ladies."

"You really are friends with everybody," I smirk, with a tinge of jealousy.

"Don't you dare start. I don't want to regret helping you. Let's go ask for the microfilm."

I've always been in love with those scenes in movies where a character goes into a library and asks for old newspapers and searches through microfilm copies. Pages going by superfast on the screen as they move some buttons until it abruptly stops and some relevant piece of information is revealed. The coolest thing ever, but I wouldn't even know how to ask for them or how to use one of the machines. Andrea does. And she's let me tag along. Cool. She has her thick black glasses on, hair freshly buzzed, wearing a white T-shirt, jeans, and black suspenders. Gosh, she's so beautiful. I can't help but notice. Don't judge me, okay? I love my ghost girl, but I still have eyes.

It's called restraint. Look it up.

I document everything with my phone, both for my vlog and for hers. We'll need to get Ernestina's permission to air all this, though. If she doesn't want to be the main character of our story, then I'll be in trouble with Andrea after all the work she's doing. I want them to meet. So, even if we can't turn all these efforts into podcasts, at least Andrea will know I'm not crazy and see I've moved on. Just like her. If she finds Ernestina's name, her family, I think it's only fair that she's the one to deliver the news.

"Do we have any idea of the time frame we're talking about here?" Andrea asks.

"I have reason to believe this spirit's favorite song was 'The Man Who Sold the World,' so I guess she must've been a teen around the time it was released? Or maybe it was popular again for some reason. Whatever the case, she couldn't have lived before it was released."

"Why do you have reason to . . ." She looks at me suspiciously. "Never mind."

Andrea makes a quick search online.

" 'The Man Who Sold the World' was released by David Bowie in 1970, so we'll start with missing persons from there. But honestly, it seems like way too wide a timeframe. We'll be here for days if we don't narrow it down a little."

"Yes, and her hair . . . It's bleached. But only two stripes at the front. Definitely not a 70s hairstyle."

SPOOKY LOVERS

"Two thin stripes? Well, that's the 90s for you. Nirvana's *MTV Unplugged* aired in 94, and they performed a very depressing cover of the song, so it tracks."

"You are like a Wiki page. You know that, right?"

It would be easier to ignore her looks if she were dumb—just saying.

"Yeah, I do. She was local, you believe?"

"Yep, she must have lived in this city or close enough. And she was around twenty-five years old. No less than twenty, for sure. No more than thirty, I think."

"That's still a hell of a lot of women in their twenties missing . . . Anything else that would help me narrow down this absurdly long and depressing list? For all their naïveté, the 90s were dark, cariño."

"Well . . . she must have disappeared during a party . . . She's wearing a black, long tulle gown, according to the witnesses, you know. And she likes . . . huevos rotos." I chuckle.

"Likes?"

"Liked. Sorry. Liked, past. Someone asked on a Ouija board . . ."

Oh, shit. Watch your tongue, girl.

"Let's see what we can do with that very useless information . . . You're very lucky I'm a genius, you know?"

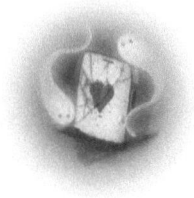

"That's her!" I jump out of my seat.

"You sure?" Andrea asks while I look closer at the screen.

We've been looking at pictures of missing women from the 90s for over an hour. It's heartbreaking. These are the ones that were never found. Las Otras.

Some are probably alive somewhere, living a new life. Some might still be barely and regrettably alive inside a basement or shed on some weirdo's property. But most are probably already dead, killed in the first hours after their disappearance, wept over but never found. Their families probably have some kind of unspoken, fantasized, terrible, terrible hope.

And finally, a familiar face. That's Ernestina, for sure. I could recognize that smile a mile away. She has something different about her, though. It's like seeing twins. They do look alike, but their eyes tell them apart. Their experiences, their personalities, differ.

"Yes, one hundred percent."

"Her name was Lola. She was training to be a librarian. She went missing on the fiftieth anniversary of this library, actually. It was that fundraiser I told you about. The council wanted to close this one; it was too big, too old. But the community came together, raised money and awareness about the importance of public libraries, the historical importance of this building . . . They saved the library that night, the same night she went missing. This is only thirty minutes away from the graveyard where you say they've seen her? Oh, look, it was a masquerade ball. Like the one they're having this weekend."

Andrea shows me another picture. Ernestina's family must've taken it before she left for the ball. She's standing in front of a staircase in a faded 90s film photograph. She's smiling, but looks embarrassed by the way she's holding her own hands. You can't really see her face because of the lace masque.

"The universe."

"What?" Andrea takes her glasses off and looks at me.

"Here, the theme of the ball," I reply, pointing at the screen, pretending I just read it instead of putting the pieces together because of the dress. "Across the Universe was the theme."

Aww, *Lola*. It really suits her. A librarian in training. Knowing who she is for certain might get us closer to catching the man who killed her and discarded her as trash. Maybe getting to know Lola will point us in the right direction to stop him from doing it again to other women.

"Okay, disclosure time, nena. I'm certain that there's something you're not telling me. So, how can you be so sure? Did you witness this woman's murder when you were a child? See someone taking her away? Because then we really need to go to the cops." Andrea's voice is very serious now. She's in full-pro mode, and she won't let me get away with anything less than the truth.

"I'm afraid that, in this case, seeing is believing. And you wouldn't buy a word I'd say about this. So, you can see for yourself, if you like. Can we print all that?"

CHAPTER VI

ERNESTINA

A vra left this morning. After getting inside of my killer's mind, we didn't need Spooky Lovers so we could hug each other, kiss each other. We merged as one. I turned to dust and let her breathe me in. Exhale me. I infected her body like a virus. I expanded inside her skin. I reproduced in her cells. I was a million spectacles and one consciousness. I was her moaning and the spark of her orgasm. All her love for me managed to calm my nerves a bit. The energy between us is so soothing. It's weird having these two different ways to be physical with each other. Both are amazing and serve two different purposes. Touching her, dissolving inside of her, lights up all my nerves like a Christmas tree, pure electricity that allows me to imagine my heart beating. While being inside Spooky Lovers is like watching a movie . . . It's nice, but it's a secondhand feeling. Filtered. Tamed. Pleasurable, but also conventional.

When she woke up this morning, she had a text from her friend Andrea agreeing to meet today. She's the person helping her out with my case. Together, Avra hopes they will be able to crack it and that I will know who I am, who I was, all by the time the dark falls tonight. The mere thought of it makes me uneasy. Time drags and seems not to pass at all. What will change once I know? Will I remember? Vanish into thin air? Discover why I am still tethered to this world?

I hate being trapped here in the cemetery, unable to help or to make time pass faster. In all fairness, I've never tried leaving the graveyard, so I don't really know if I'm truly confined here or not. There wasn't anywhere else I wanted to be before I met Avra. I've walked to the cemetery gates on several occasions, stood there looking at the road, at my ravens flying over it, disappearing in the distance, and coming back, but I was unable to move then. First of all, I was frightened of people seeing me and hurting me, but there was also the fear of melting away when trying to cross the rusty gates, of disappearing for good. The void's terrifying. Maybe because I don't even sleep now, I can't even picture having my thoughts disconnected, not being present.

Hell is nothingness.

I just wish I could help her somehow. What a useless thing I am when I'm not able to remember anything but little details, sensations. Vague, incomplete thoughts. Snippets of songs. Aftertastes of food that I can't name.

Maybe if I concentrate hard enough, I can remember the other girls who were roaming in his mind while I was inside him. Maybe if I can see some of them, something useful . . . Avra would be able to help them too. At least give some closure to their families. If they'd been found, he would've been stopped.

I can't explain it, but I feel him. I wouldn't know how to explain how I feel my hands or my mouth, but they are there. So is he now as well, and he is not done.

I go back to Ernestina's tomb and hover over it. Closing my eyes, I descend, seeking that special kind of darkness to immerse completely in my own thoughts.

In his thoughts. In the ones I tried to evade. In the ones I forced myself to avoid.

If I push myself a little harder, I might breach the fabric of reality that separates us. I might be able to explore his mind freely without being subjected to my own murder and . . . the rest. I descend to the ground where he left me. Not even a speck of light or hope is down here.

Breathe in, breathe out, relax.

I don't focus on my body or on what it suffered when he killed me. I focus on those revolting feelings that swarmed like maggots devouring rotten flesh inside him. The hunger. The lust. The fast heartbeat.

The sweat on his forehead.

The tensing muscles in his abdomen.

I push myself deeper, forcing myself to look.

To feel.

Most importantly, to enjoy.

I moan as I welcome those physical sensations, the gratification, the spasms. I fall down the rabbit hole and come out the other side, where the light is dim and the air smells like dust and books.

I did it. Hell yeah, I did it.

Am I in a memory? Is this happening now? I can see his hands. He is reading. It's a big, heavy book. He's wearing white gloves and using tweezers to handle it. I have to pay attention to everything. Every little detail. There's a glass of water on the table, close to him. If this were a memory, I wouldn't be able to do anything, to force him to do anything. I concentrate really hard on the glass of water, on my thirst. My tongue is stiff, my lips chapped. Desertlike thirst.

You are thirsty, you bastard. Come on. The water is just there.

Drink.

He reaches out for the glass and downs a big gulp of water.

I sigh, relieved. I'm inside of his mind, and I might've saved myself from the pain of going through anyone's murder. I wouldn't be able to handle it. Watching myself was one thing, but being trapped inside him while he kills someone unable to help them? That would be my definition of going through hell.

A clock rings and he stops reading. The tediousness inside him turns sour. He doesn't want to leave this book, but duty calls, and if he wants to keep living the life he enjoys, then he has to compromise on things like this. I'm completely inside his mind. But like riding a bike, I'm afraid I need some training to effectively navigate here. He drinks some more water, closes the book, and leaves the glove on the table next to it. We're moving.

We're facing the wall, though there's a passage here. This is no regular door. How's he opening it? He must've done this so many times that he doesn't even need to look or think about the process. A hidden mechanism, a code? Maldita sea.

The light is brighter on the other side of the door, but not by that much. The air's warm, and the humidity conditions are absolutely perfect. Dark wooden bookshelves. Silence except for his shoes against the floor tiles. We are in a library now.

Oh, I . . . know this place. Is the déjà vu mine, or is his familiarity with it infecting me? He carries a trolley with books, bestsellers that he despises. The hatred toward everyone here tastes like damp earth in the mouth. He stops. Something's caught his attention. His muscles tense. His body reacts like he's found an oasis in the desert. Just like he felt when he met me.

Wait, is that . . . Avra?

It can't be. No. *No*. Please no. My voice echoes inside his head. A hundred eyes are looking for me now. I feel them coming, like smelling rain in the air.

There's no doubt: that's Avra with Andrea. They're laughing, checking something next to a printer. My own love for Avra, ignited by fear he might hurt her, mixes with the hunger inside him. I try not to feel. I try to get all that love back inside my ribcage. But he can't take his eyes off them now. Determination builds inside him. It bubbles. It's pressing. A plan begins to develop. He *knows* Andrea.

No. *No.*

I scream and his eyes finally find me.

He's looking into a bookshelf with a glass door. He's seen me. He smirks and moves closer. Like a distorted mirror, the shelf shows both of us.

Now, I'm no longer in the library but in a blank space. A negative space. There's only me. Then a voice at my back.

"I love a good ghost story. I never thought I'd get to live one." His voice is harsh, but honey-like. Something inside me reacts, but not in the way I would've expected. I used to... love that voice. There's pain and grief. Love and heartache. The aftertaste of fear.

"I often wondered. You were so young, so full of life. If anyone had unfinished business, it must've been you." He's facing me now, caressing my cheeks with the back of his hand. I tremble like a leaf. "You know, I used to stay awake at night at first, waiting for you to haunt me. Not afraid of it, but aching for it. I wanted to see you again. To feel you again."

He's so close to me I can sense the warmth of his body. His smell of wood, dust, and cigarettes. He grabs my neck. This pain I know.

"It's so good to see you again. But not like this. Not inside my head, tse tse. I'll be more than happy to kill you again if you ever try that again. I'd love to. You were my best."

CHAPTER VII
AVRA

The printer spits news article after news article about Lola's disappearance. Unfortunately for her, some other gruesome crime caught the attention of the public, and she was soon forgotten. Except for those who loved her, I guess. The family in the pictures. I go to turn on my phone's notifications again. I have thirty-five missed calls from a number comprised of letters and numbers and signs. Oh. A hundred messages on Spooky Lovers. Most of them are different versions of *Where the hell are you?* and *Get the fuck out of there now* and *Damn Avra, get the damned phone*. What happened? I try calling the odd number, but obviously that doesn't work. I text Ernestina to let her know we're okay and we're on our way, but my phone battery dies.

"Oh, mierda. We need to leave now," I urge Andrea.

"But it's not done printing," she protests.

"I don't care, we have enough. Let's go, coño! Give me the keys."

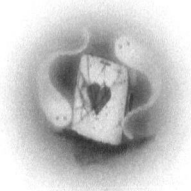

I drive us to the graveyard. I try not to rush or be too frenzied in front of Andrea, but I'm worried about Ernestina. She's never been the jealous type or been this hectic before. I'm sure it's nothing. Or at least I hope so. I'm eager to tell her that her real name is Lola. And Andrea's eager to know what this is all about. I know she's excited, and I can hear the gears in her head plotting the podcast episode.

"Here?" she asks when we stop at the cemetery gates. "You must be joking. What are we going to do now, ghost hunt?"

"No, there's no need to hunt... Come on. Pack everything."

When we cross the gates, there are no flowers, and the ravens seem angry. They caw and fly menacingly over our heads. Oh, no.

It *was* something.

"Maybe we should leave," Andrea suggests, as she turns on the lantern of her mobile phone.

"There used to be some kind of... warm lighting, I don't know... Maybe wait for a second in the car. I'll call you to let you know when to come in."

"This is insane. I don't think you should go alone."

"Oh, come on, you know I do this all the time. Five minutes, okay?"

"Five minutes, then I'm coming for you."

When I reach the church doors, Ernestina's *mad*.

"You are *late*! You should've been here hours ago!"

"Yes, Ghosty, I know, but we fou—"

"I don't care, I was worried sick. I thought you were dead!" Her voice breaks.

SPOOKY LOVERS

"Why would I be dead? I was just researching with Andrea, as I told you this morning when I left."

"I saw you! Through his eyes!" She collapses on the floor, crying desperately.

"How could you? Ernestina, you are not making any sense now." What is she talking about? Yesterday, she managed to see her own death through his eyes, and suddenly, she knows what goes on in his head.

"You don't understand! You are in danger now!"

"How? How can I be in danger? Tell me," I beg her, trying to kiss her hands that vanish at my touch.

"He saw you. He saw you. I was inside of him, and he was looking at you. You got too close. I don't know who he is, but he will hurt you, like he hurt me," she cries. "I don't want you to investigate any more about my past. I don't need to know, and to hell with the others if you are in danger . . ."

"We already know everything about your past. And we'll help las Otras, too." Andrea peeks through the door, holding the news clips. Pale. Shivering.

Well, she's just seen a ghost for the first time.

CHAPTER VIII

ERNESTINA

L ola.
    Lo-la.
Dolores.
Lo.

It all feels foreign. It doesn't really bring any memories forward, but the woman in that picture is me. There's no mistaking it.

That's my dress. My face. My smile. But not my eyes. I don't recognize myself as that girl, full of life and a future, with that name. There are pictures of Lola's parents I don't recognize either. I'm disappointed. This numbness wasn't exactly what I'd pictured. Memories should've flown through with these gates opened. It's infuriating. I put my love in danger for nothing, for more of this nothingness.

"Sorry, I don't remember anything." I sigh, giving the folder back to Andrea. She's not shaking anymore.

"It's okay. We know a fair number of things about you now. Do you want me to go over them? See if something sparks a memory?" Andrea asks tenderly. Fear has left room for pity.

I hate pity.

"Sure."

Andrea grabs the news clips. Avra looks at her with admiration, and I'm sure she finds her incredibly attractive still, despite the breakups and the heartache. Who wouldn't? She's incredibly beautiful in both conventional and unconventional ways. But when Avra looks at me, there's something different. She might desire Andrea, but she loves me. Those eyes, her gestures, the way she talks to me and her. There's no mistaking it.

I'm concerned about Avra; she makes my heart bloom with bright flowers, and I would protect her with my life . . . with . . . I would do anything in my power to save her if the time came. I can't shake the feeling that *his* desire for her was ignited by my love for her, as though he could feel it when I was inside him.

"As we told you, when you were alive, your name was Dolores. But according to this statement your sister gave, everyone called you *Lola*. Both your parents, Alberto and Susana, were alive when you disappeared. We haven't tried locating them yet. But it wasn't so long ago, so they should be fine—fingers crossed. You had a sister, Sara. She's three years older. She owns a craft supply store we found easily online. She's pretty successful and even has a weekly streaming show about crafting. You wanted to be a librarian and were training to do so. The night you went missing, you attended a fundraising ball, and that's where we think he . . . killed you."

There's nothing, no reaction. Not even a longing, an ache. The void of death and no more. I shake my head.

"Nothing, Ghosty? Try concentrating on their names, maybe? Their faces? Andrea, show her the pictures again."

There are my parents, holding each other in a magazine clipping. I didn't even make the cover. The woman cries on the man's shoulder. They do bear some resemblance to my features, and that's undeniable.

Come on. Focus on the smell.

I close my eyes. The flowers. The itchy tulle. The lace of the masque against my nose, smelling like new fabric and hot glue. Then, when that vague sensation of having something on the tip of my tongue fills me, I open my eyes again, trying to lock that onto the faces in the magazine. The feeling dissipates as soon as I see their faces, though. It doesn't match the crying face of Lola's mother. Another girl is standing next to them with my picture: my sister. A thinner version of me, with pursed lips and red eyes; she had been crying and was trying to hide her pain, pretending she was strong. There's no direct link between me and her, no retraceable path from Ernestina to Lola.

I'm still just me. The Marigold Girl. A ghost with no memories and no family.

There are others in the picture, those who participated in the searches, who wanted to help. They might've been Lola's extended family and friends. I look at them with curiosity. Did she fancy any of them? Were any of them the Raven Man who killed me? If my family's love doesn't bring back anything, maybe that naïve love of the first spins of the dance will do it. I focus on those others.

"That's him," I shout at the top of my lungs as if I've been stung by a bee. My killer's right behind my parents, sitting on the table they set for people joining in the search for me. This is the flooding I'd hoped for. His smile calmed me down on my first day. The first time his fingers casually caressed mine when handing me a rare edition of *A Room of One's Own*. The coffee he used to bring for me in the mornings. The taste of the chocolate we hid under the counter and snuck bites of. The nights spent fantasizing about him. His lips. His hands on my body.

I shiver. I wanted him, loved him. He was a kind man. Turns out he was just pretending. And I fell for it like an idiot. I bought it all. Every word, every tender look. Loving him was wrong because he was my mentor, twenty years older than me, divorced. When he asked me to be his date for the ball and asked for me to keep it a secret, to act like we were just friends in front of others . . . I didn't really tell anyone about my hopes for the night. He'd made it clear he felt the same. It was going to be our night, the night we shared everything, the night of our first kiss. That's why the dress and the masque were so important. I sprayed my mother's perfume on my dress for him. Maybe my silence protected him from being scrutinized. My killer turned me into an accomplice to my own murder.

I feel the darkness falling around me, but this time, I fight back. No way you're taking me now.

"The librarian?" Avra asks. The question helps me tether to reality. Then I remember being inside him, desiring Avra.

"I told you. I told you he was watching you in the library."

"No, no, it's impossible. He's not the most cheerful person in the world, but he can't be a killer. I've known him ever since I started going there to do my research. He's a nice man."

"We both know the worst ones are those who know how to fake niceness, cielo." Avra takes the stack of papers and goes through them. "Yeah, his name is Gabriel Cuervo. He was your mentor in the library and then led the volunteer search. Look, there's even an interview with him."

His gray eyes cross my mind, and I feel dizzy as I read the words on the paper she's handed me.

"Lola is destined for great things. She has a light of her own. Let's pray she'll come back home safe and sound, so we can continue to live under her shine."

The softness of the raven's feathers on my neck makes my back stiff. The taste of strawberry lipstick. Salty tears. My mother's perfume. It all mingles in my mind with those words.

"You shine, bright as a star," he said in my ear as he greeted me the night of the ball. I was over the moon.

If ghosts could faint, I would. Knowing that he was my mentor, that I had fallen for him, ate up all his lies, fills me with anger. He was supposed to take care of me, to teach me, to guide me. And he chose to cut my life short instead. Just for that few seconds his orgasm lasted? That was the worth of my whole life, my whole future?

"Ok, Ghosty, now you tell us what you know."

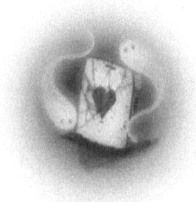

Andrea sits in silence on my tombstone, on Ernestina's tombstone. She's no longer pale, and she has gotten used to my cold and jasmine scent. I've been holding my lover's hand the whole time, or at least trying to, getting the tinkling feeling on the back of my spine as my hand disappears inside her flesh. I told Andrea everything I could remember from the last time I relived my death. Avra already knows it—she was here when it happened—so she looks distracted, thoughtful.

I half expect Andrea to accuse me of lying. I'm ready to fight her tooth and nail to convince her that he is my killer, that he's the bastard who took my future away from me, my light, my chance to kiss Avra's lips for real. But Andrea is listening. In silence. Not a single interruption on her part. She isn't drifting away. She's focused and present, nodding and trying not to show her true feelings, the sadness, the pity, the rage. She does a poor job at it, but I welcome the reactions.

"That's all I remember. I'm sorry I can't give you more details, and I'm sorry he is someone you trusted. I'm ashamed I trusted him too. I fancied him, like an idiot..."

There's a moment of silence. My whole body trembles as I look to Avra, looking for clues as to what's going to happen now. She nods, reassuring me. Then, Andrea stands, comes toward us, and kneels before me. She's about to hold my shoulders when she realizes she won't be able to, stops midair, and just looks at me, dead serious, in the eyes.

"Don't you ever apologize for him again. Are you listening? Never again. I've been doing my job long enough to know that people only show us the face they want us to see. Gabriel being nice to me is only one side of him, and it means nothing. I would never doubt you. I'm okay. You gave us the most useful insight of all. We know where you are buried and who did that to you. You are not one of las Otras anymore. You have a name. And we'll take you back to your family."

"So, we know who the bastard is. Now what? We go to the police?" Avra asks Andrea.

"Not yet."

"What do you mean 'not yet'? We can't wait. He might kill someone soon if we don't stop him!" Avra protests.

"Right, let's say we go to the cops now. What do you propose we tell them? 'You see, my ex-girlfriend here is dating a ghost woman, and she has told us who killed her and where she's buried'?" Andrea snaps. Avra sighs. "Not only would it not do her any good, but it would most likely kill my reputation and get you into real trouble if you go around telling the authorities that you're dating ghosts."

Silence falls between the two of them. Dreadful and full of horrible notions, it must be broken, and so I say:

"She has a point, and I don't want any of you getting in any more danger. He's dangerous, and he's got the hunger again. We need a plan, a better one."

Andrea stands and walks in circles like you might expect someone to do in a detective cartoon. Neither Avra nor I interrupt her thoughts. Instead, we look at each other. Avra's eyes are reassuring. We don't need words now to express how much we care, how much we would love to make the oppressing feelings of the other go away. Did I ever feel like this when I was alive? A feeling so strong should definitely accompany you to the other side if you were ever lucky enough to experience it, so my guess now is that Lola never really fell in love. She had this longing for Gabriel, this fantasy of him being the one. But it doesn't resemble what Avra makes me feel.

Suddenly, Andrea stops in her tracks, looks at us, and waits until we pay attention to her.

"We need evidence, real physical evidence. Prints. Tracks. Bite marks."

Avra sighs and rests her head in her hands. Am I missing something? That actually sounds good. Why would she react as if it was a dreadful idea?

"We need to find las Otras, his trophies if he had any. We track the bodies down, and then we make an anonymous call to the police. Drop all we know at their doorstep. Even the most incompetent of them all would be able to put the pieces together once we serve them on a golden plate."

"Okay, but where do we start?" I ask, happy to know there's a plan in place.

They both turn to look at me with the same bleak look Avra had a minute ago.

"You'll have to see him kill las Otras."

CHAPTER IX

ERNESTINA

"No, there must be another way," I reply, feeling a knot in my throat, trying to find a way out of this, although I know Andrea is right. Sweet Jesus, how I hate that she's right . . .

Find las Otras they say. Go into him again, into his memories. See them being slaughtered. Like it's that easy. Like I will be just watching a movie of their deaths instead of feeling each and every last one of his nerves as he takes the life away from them. Like I won't be feeling the blood pumping in their veins in the palms of his hands. Like I won't taste them. Eat their fear.

But they're right, I have to look.

"I wish I could think of a better way, believe me, but . . . Wouldn't you want to use it if we had access to video recordings of him doing it?"

I nod as a reply.

"This is the closest we have to that. Only . . . you have to . . ."

"Yeah, look until the very end . . . I figured."

Until the very end to know where he buried them. Name them. Find them. Las Otras. Are they ghosts, too? Am I the only one? If so, why? If I look, maybe we can get evidence and get the police to follow the right leads, help them connect the dots. Fucking connect them for them if we need to.

Andrea and Avra walk with me toward Ernestina's grave, my burial site. The forgotten piece of land where Gabriel Cuervo dumped me. I go down into the darkness again. I have to get inside his mind, inside his very own private library. Into his twisted mind, the memories he treasures. Like the trophies he got from us, from me and las Otras.

The dark eats me, and I focus. I push. I feel. I'm in.

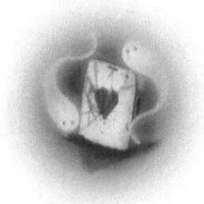

I'm in a dark hallway. It's the day of the ball, my ball. The day of my death. There I am, dancing, alive. The candles flickering. The string quartet of women dressed in tuxedos. The planets made of cardboard hanging from the ceiling. I've never seen it from this side. It was a gorgeous ball. Everyone looks ravishing; it really was the stuff of dreams.

But no, not this night. This night, I know plenty well, thank you.

I walk down the hall, ignoring the dancing figures around me. The masques and the sound of high heels against the tiles. Running from the smell of my mother's perfume, I look around for a path to follow through into the next memory. There's a door at the end of the hallway. It's wet, water running from it, making a puddle on the floor. I turn right and get to it. It's cold. Black seaweed grows around it. Cursed morsels. Dreadful fishbones. The door is heavy, black. I push, letting out a cry, until it finally gives.

SPOOKY LOVERS

I'm inside the library.

It's a dark winter morning. Rain falls against the windows. People wear winter clothes. A woman walks into the library. She's soaking wet. But it seems like she finds it amusing. She's not from here. Her features tell me the sun is the norm where she lives. She doesn't know how ever-changing the weather is here. Gabriel is looking at her from behind the counter, bored, despising everyone in the room until she catches his attention. Her hair is dark, and her smile broad and sincere. There's something about her that makes him think of me. The way she moves her hands to tie her wet hair up, how she makes eye contact with him with playful eyes. Not flirting, not sexy, she just feels like... a dork, all wet from the sudden rain, with everyone looking at her.

"I'm sorry. I'm afraid you'll have to go mopping the floor behind me." She's naïve and sincere, extroverted and funny, the kind of woman who wouldn't notice any possible innuendos in a conversation.

And the hunger strikes. He remembers how good I felt and wonders if it would be half as good a second time. He pictures her mouth still, her eyes covered by a white veil. The feeling that I could have been friends with this woman makes me sad. I weep inside his mind, ruining his memories, tainting them with sorrow. Something tinkles behind me. He's sensing that sorrow, and he knows damned well it's not his. He's sensed me. He knows I'm here. I wonder what he can do to stop it. Could he? I move forward, pushing through layers of her visits to the library and snippets of conversations.

Her name is Irene. She's a student from the south of Italy.

He's a patient man. The net he's weaving looks a lot like flirting, like he's courting her. He's only preparing her for the slaughter, like feeding a little lamb to fatten it.

I turn to the coffee corner where he has invited her to have one of those hideous coffees from the machine, and the library's turned into a small restaurant.

Wait. I've been here. I recognize the tiny wooden tables with paper tablecloths. The small, white, old plates. The air smells like chopped onions and boiling chicken broth.

Huevos rotos.

Lola loved their huevos rotos. It's a small traditional restaurant, not far from the library. I used to come here with my sister. They reminded us of the ones my abuela used to cook when we were hungover teens. I brought him here one day after work. I mustered the courage to ask him to join me. A treat for being such a good mentor to me, a hope that he'd make a move. Like time collapsing in over itself, we are having dinner at the same table they are having dinner. Years apart, yet the same. She likes him. I liked him. He's charming that way.

But he doesn't want this version of either of us. I push forward to get away from my sitting with him, looking at him with dove eyes.

I'm in his living room now. He likes his decoration minimal. Irene's drinking wine on the couch. She's enjoying the evening. It's not their first date. Why didn't they investigate him when she disappeared? Just another foreign student gone wild and missing? Her laughing mortifies him until he reaches the point of not being able to fake being the nice librarian anymore. He's sick of hearing it. He wants her mute. Blank eyes, the light leaving them, a white veil covering the black pupil. He remembers my dead face, my limp body, and the hunger turns unbearable.

First, it was disbelief that caught her. Then fear. I keep looking through his eyes, crying, my heart breaking, infecting this memory, ruining it for him. I keep looking through his eyes, in case he makes a mistake.

I keep looking, until she's nothing more than a ruined toy on the carpet under the dining table.

He regrets doing it in his own house. He has to be smarter next time, though he's sure she hasn't told anyone about their date. He checks her phone, just in case. Nothing. He told her he couldn't date the library patrons. He could get in trouble. She didn't say anything to anyone to protect his job.

SPOOKY LOVERS

He doesn't have close neighbors. He places her body in his car, as he did with me, but he doesn't take her to the graveyard—too much work. I pay close attention to the signs along the way. A turn from the main road onto a dirt one. He dumps her body in the swamp, tied to his spare wheel.

I'm suddenly submerged in his fantasy of her body floating like a delicate flower. My body entangled in her hair. Bony fingers eaten by fish clawing at my ankles. I look down, and her fleshless face grins at me with eyes wide open. White. Sad. Lifeless.

Like mine were.

That's it.

Then, amid the excruciating illusion of drowning, I realize I'm already dead.

Water can't fill my lungs because this is all inside my head. Or rather, inside his. Fishes swimming frantically block the sun. I spin past them toward the light again, leaving Irene's memory behind.

When I reach the surface of the water memory, instead of going upward, I fall through a door. A hard concrete door on the floor. All my bones crack and hurt against the cold, firm surface.

"Disappointed your little trick with the water didn't work, huh? It's infuriating for you, isn't it? Not being in command!" I shout inside this dark, empty room in his head. Let him find me; I don't give a damn anymore.

There's nothing worse left for him to do to me.

I stomp on the concrete floor as hard as I can. The sound resonates, forcing the whole empty room to vibrate. His head hurts.

"I have so much pain ready for you," I murmur as I stomp again. Harder. Yet again. The floor cracks beneath my feet. Like Alice in her wonderland, I fall.

And fall.

And fall.

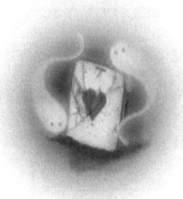

I close my eyes, and when I open them, I'm looking out from behind his again—in a supermarket. We're waiting in line.

It's kind of funny to imagine him doing all this common stuff. These boring, regular, everyday-life things like grocery shopping or brushing his teeth, paying taxes or having family dinners. How can he? With all these dark memories inside his head, with our corpses roaming around in his mind, how can he focus on choosing a new brand of cereal? Keep going on like it's nothing? Like he hasn't destroyed entire worlds with his own hands? The same hands that now hold a bag of bread and a bottle of white wine.

The cashier looks just like me, like Lola. An older version of her, if she'd been given the chance to age. Gray bags under her eyes and calloused hands. The similarities stir the desire inside him. It's been long enough—too long—since he took Irene.

The itch is back.

A million questions pop into his head: What does her skin taste like? Would it be as good as it was when he bit me? She smells of fresh sweat, cheap deodorant, and cigarettes. Irene was a disappointment, in some ways, because she didn't taste anything like me, not remotely. Her body hadn't been as welcoming either. *It's never going to be as good as the first time,* he fears.

Nevertheless, he has to try again.

He's friendly. Charming. A handsome man dedicated to his mission. Discovering her work schedule doesn't take long. Her shifts match his perfectly. It was bound to happen.

SPOOKY LOVERS

He goes shopping there every day. Just small things. Silly stuff he obviously doesn't need. It adds to his charm that he's a bit clumsy that way. It's easier to paint himself as harmless if he buys two carrots and shrugs guiltily with a tender smile that cries, *I'm here just for you.*

And this new girl, she falls for it. She smiles every time he crosses the door. Flattery is written all over her face. It's just a matter of patience. Gabriel Cuervo's a master of that. If he weren't, he would've been caught already. He has to be careful with the timing. He has to choose them wisely, so she'll be blamed.

She went out with strangers.
How many men did she have?
She was too flirtatious.

Irene was all *that*. Authorities will pass over her case as an inevitable catastrophe. A misfortune bound to happen to a reckless woman.

One day, he pretends to look at the name tag on the cashier's uniform as if he didn't know her name since the very first day she started working there.

"Thank you, er, Adela."

She blushes, unaware that the innocence in her face has just sealed her fate.

Then, it's just a matter of waiting until the opportunity presents itself.

A late shift. A broken-down car. A car *he* broke. And a Good Samaritan, just happening to pass by.

Adela trusts him. Why wouldn't she? Gabriel's a friendly man from the neighborhood, someone she's been harmlessly flirting with for months. Small talk, hands barely touching, complacent smiles. She gets inside his car without a second thought. No one witnesses her getting in. He makes sure of it. For the rest of the world, Adela's just vanishing into thin air, leaving a broken-down vehicle and a bunch of questions behind. When he parks the car in the middle of nowhere, she's not scared. She smiles. Adela leans in to kiss him.

And that's it.

Adela's one and only sin that night.

He strangles her in his car. He can't wait or help himself—and all just because she's kissed him. He doesn't like being kissed. He doesn't desire warm skin. A woman's will, her desire—it's all disgusting for him.

I try to look the other way as she gasps for air, kicking and damaging the interior of his car. He will take care of that later. The mechanic will buy whatever bullshit he comes up with to explain the damage. They will laugh together about that wild animal he hit with his car, then tried to rescue. *Don't tell anyone, but I've been having fawn for dinner. Nothing comes close to that taste.*

It takes a while, but finally she's motionless. Gone. Eyes open toward the dark sky.

That's how he craves her body: a mere empty doll. He takes her right there in his car. The hunger doesn't allow him to wait, to go somewhere else.

There's a construction site not far from where they parked. He knows the owner of the company; they have dinner together from time to time. They were college buddies. Gabriel knows he won't ask too many questions if an old friend asks for a favor. *There's something I need gone for good, you know?* The workers will dump concrete upon her remains tomorrow, and no one will ever find her.

He takes a lock of her hair and a piece of her uniform.

She's still there, trapped in gray amber, stood upon by hundreds of feet, unaware of her presence, of the rotting corpse of a missing woman under their offices.

So, this is who we were. Who we are now.

Three dead women.

Three corpses without graves.

"I've seen enough, bastard," I say as I explode in a million particles, a million golden, salty tears inside his mind.

SPOOKY LOVERS

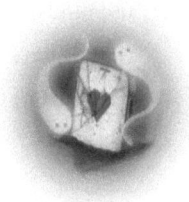

Avra's red, puffy eyes avoid mine. Andrea keeps hers locked onto the floor. A mobile phone trembles in her hand. A red dot blinks on it.

"What's that for? Were you recording this?"

"Yes. Maybe you didn't mean to, but you've been telling us what you . . . what *he* was doing all the way through . . ." Andrea answers, then looks at me. "In great detail."

"Have I? I . . . I didn't mean to," I stutter.

"It was like hearing his internal monologue. I'm afraid it was quite disturbing." Andrea stops the recording, giving me a commiserating smile. She walks toward Avra and puts her hand on her shoulder. Avra grabs it and squishes it hard, nodding, and Andrea leaves us alone, carrying away with her that sad smile that freezes my heart.

"Are you okay, babe? Because I'm okay." I look at her tenderly, hiding the lie as best I can. Not well enough, by the looks of it.

Avra shakes her head, cleans her tears, and takes a deep breath, still unable to face me. "Look, I know very damn well it wasn't you talking . . . But it's one thing to have you tell us about Gabriel Cuervo killing two women, and a whole different one to hear you saying those awful things as if they were happening in front of us, and . . . you were enjoying them. I just hate it when you are inside of him. Your eyes are not your eyes. His hunger, his desire, his lust peeks behind them. I'm sorry I feel like this. I know it's not your fault." She musters the courage to turn her head and look at me.

I'm at a loss for words. What can I say to make it all go away? I'd give anything to have met her in another life, in the next one, instead of in this impasse between light and darkness, full of dangers and monsters, but here we are... I open my mouth to speak, to comfort her, but I have nothing to offer.

"Was it worth it, at least? Did I give you enough information to find las Otras?" I ask, trying to change the conversation to focus on the present moment.

"Honestly, I have no clue. Andrea's the expert in these kinds of investigative endeavors. I wouldn't know what to do with any of the information you... *he* gave us." Avra stands up, walking away from me. "I'll go get her, see if she's found something useful, so we can get this over with as soon as possible."

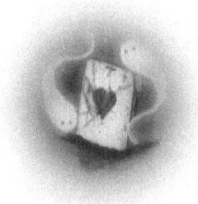

Andrea's going over the recorded session from her cellphone. She's taking notes, listening. She's nodding and pursing her lips with a dozen tabs open in her computer's browser. When she plays the audio again, I'm utterly shocked. *Is that my voice?* It can't be. It's deep and harsh, without emotion—too controlled. That voice talks about what I saw in the first person, giving away details I wouldn't have shared with them had I had the chance to redact my experience for Avra and Andrea afterward.

I place my fingers over Avra's hand, just enough to feel her warmth. She smiles as the hairs on her arm stand up. My energy has that effect on her, just like hers lightens me up. We both smile. As we wait for Andrea to study everything, we stay in the corner of the church.

"I love you," I murmur in her ear for the very first time. This feels like the right moment to say it. A way to wash away all our pain.

"I love you," she whispers back with teary eyes. "I wish I could hold your hands or kiss you."

"I know, my love, and I'm sorry . . . Maybe I shouldn't have touched that damned phone . . ."

Andrea closes her computer and stands, interrupting my apologies for dragging Avra into my own private hell.

"Amigas," she calls us with a stack of papers in her hands. "I have news."

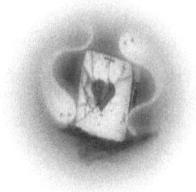

Andrea's face tells me this isn't going to be good, and my mood sinks.

"Ernestina, I'm really sorry you had to go through that terrible experience, but none of this data is really helpful to get to the police right now."

Those are *precisely* the words I didn't want to hear.

"I did it for nothing?"

"Not for nothing, no. I've located the sites where the bodies are, I think, more or less. There could be a couple of different options for Water Lady, but I'm sure about our Concrete Girl. Digging them up is not going to be easy, and any physical evidence is long gone in the water and because of the corrosive effect of concrete . . ."

"Irene and Adela," I say, looking at the floor.

"What?" Andrea looks at me as if she'd been snagged from a dream.

"Their names are not *Concrete Lady* or *Water Anything*. Their names are Irene and Adela," I reply.

"Yes, right. Sorry, I didn't mean to . . ." Andrea stops midsentence. "No excuses, you are right. I'm sorry, Er."

"Right, see? We even know their names. What's stopping us from going to the police right now, Andrea?" Avra asks, eager to move forward.

"We could go to the cops and say we are mediums, and it wouldn't be any different. We're stuck with the exact same problem as before. If one of these women were buried somewhere, we could stumble upon casually . . . But what good would that do if there's nothing to point to *him*? Trust me, I know. I've been in similar situations . . . Well, not that similar, but you know what I mean . . . The thing is, I've been here a dozen times, and it never works out well." Andrea walks around the graves with her arms folded.

I forced myself to look, and all for nothing? I endured this sacrifice for nothing? He'll do it all over again if we don't stop him, and we're not even an inch closer to getting him. My ravens fly in circles over us, cawing in desperation. Black flowers bloom beneath my feet, and poison ivy crawls over the graves.

"It's okay, Ernestina. You tried . . ." Avra looks at the birds, afraid, trying to avoid the touch of my poison ivy, then takes her fingers to her lips tenderly, looking me in the eye.

I wish I was flesh and bones so hard right now, so she could kiss me for real, so I could feel the comfort of her touch. I imitate her gesture. A knot tightens in my stomach. If we don't stop him, *she* could be next. He's determined, persistent, and he isn't used to not getting his way. A shadow of dread falls over me.

Avra *will* be next. I'm sure of it.

Andrea stops and looks at us, at the ravens, and at nature turning dark.

"Amigas, I have another idea. It was my first one, actually, but it's riskier, so I wanted to give this a try first. No offense, Er, but you can't really get hurt in there. He's already done all the harm he can to you. There's something else we could do, but it would put Avra and me on the line if we don't do it right . . ."

I have the feeling I know what she's going to say.

And I don't like it one bit.

CHAPTER X

AVRA

We're crazy.

Totally nuts.

But it all makes sense, doesn't it?

It's pretty simple really, and we should have started there instead of putting Ernestina through hell for nothing. Well, not nothing. At least now we know where las Otras' bodies are. Though, according to my expert ex-girlfriend, it's just not enough. Underwater, under a ton of concrete... Why can't anything be easy? All I ever wanted was love, a loving relationship, matching Victorian wedding dresses, and yes, I found love, better yet, LOVE in capital letters, but also a bunch of dead women and a serial killer.

We need to break into his house.

Yeah, right.

Andrea's voice sounded so matter-of-fact when she said it that it felt like those seven words had always belonged to her tongue in that particular order.

"You don't happen to remember his address, right, Ernestina?" Andrea asks.

"I don't think I was ever inside his house. This is going to sound weird, but I do remember Lola's interactions with him. Nothing about family or anyone else, but about him . . . It's all here. We always saw each other at work and at the restaurant near the library a couple of times. Never at his place."

"No big deal, we know his name and where he works. It's not going to be that difficult. And if we don't find his address online, we can always just follow him after work."

I'm horrified by the way they talk about it as if it were nothing. Are they delusional? Am I too scared? Shouldn't they be, too?

"Right, just follow the murderer home as if he's not going to see us and bury us in his garden," I half joke.

"Do you really think I won't be able to find his address?" Andrea asks, as if I had offended her whole family tree.

I throw my hands in the air and go sit in the corner of the church, to calm down and stop being a whining bitch. I need to eat something. My mother used to tell me: "When you hate everybody, eat. When you think everyone hates you, sleep."

I wish I had some donuts here.

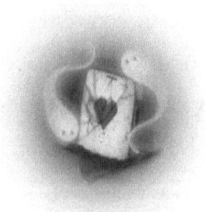

Andrea sits inside the church with the laptop on her lap.

"You know, the connection here is shitty at best. It's going to take a while with this twentieth-century internet speed . . ."

"I can help with that." Ernestina walks toward her, sits next to her, and touches the computer.

"Coño, it's even charging. That's a useful skill. Thank you."

Andrea's clearly fascinated with Ernestina and her abilities. After all these years of thinking I was crazy, she's found herself immersed in my craziness, and she's loving it. I'm not going to say, "I told you so." Knowing I was right is a good enough feeling. Although, it might slip out the next time I've had one drink too many. Would you blame me? It's been way too many years of being called Repelús Avra not to gorge on the fact that everything I said was, at the very least, reasonable.

"I got his address. For a serial murderer, you'd think he'd be more careful with his data online. He's not that smart, after all. They never are." The triumph in her voice is like a breeze of fresh air inside the dampened church. Andrea doesn't have any doubts that this is what needs to be done.

"Are you girls sure of this? I'm not even . . ." Ernestina's never looked more like a ghost than she does in this very moment. She's as pale as porcelain, more translucid than usual.

"Yeah, don't worry. We know his schedule, right? He'll be at work, and we'll be done before he comes back. We just need to take enough evidence to dump at the police station, so they do the work from there," Andrea reassures her.

"Yeah, Ghosty, easy peasy. In and out as if we had never been there, and Gabriel Cuervo will spend the rest of his Mondays locked up."

This is the first time I lie to her.

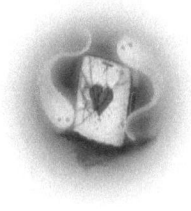

We visit the library again in the morning. They're hanging a big cardboard planet from the front door with a "75th" drawn on it with bright markers. The decorations for the next anniversary ball are almost ready. It's the opening hour, so with our coffees in hand, we try to pretend the world hasn't burned down and reshaped itself since we were here yesterday. We need to make sure he *is* here before heading to his place.

"Was the day productive, Andi?" the guard asks with a big smile.

"Oh, well, not really. That's why we have to come back today," she smiles. "We have to keep looking. It was a false alarm, I'm afraid."

"Let's keep at it, then. You forgot some copies on the printer when you left yesterday, but don't worry, I gave them to Gabi. So just go to the counter and ask him for them. He was telling me yesterday that he hasn't seen you in forever."

Andrea's fake smile turns into a dreadful grimace that she tries to hide by looking at me, sipping at her coffee, and smiling back at him before coming in.

"You're not actually thinking about asking him, right? Those documents were all about Lola," I mutter. "We just needed to see he was here and then fly to his place knowing he won't be back, and we already know that."

"We have to now; don't you think he's going to find it suspicious if we don't ask him? Like we know something? Act normal, por el amor de dios."

Gabriel Cuervo is sitting behind the counter desk, and he welcomes us with a big smile. The most charming expression one could manage. *Gosh, he's so good at this.* He leans on the counter; his pale hands contrast with the mahogany. I can't stop thinking about those huge hands around Ernestina's neck. Picturing her flying in the air in front of him, held only by these huge hands, as I saw her on our first date when she relived her death in front of me. Imagining the whole scene, I choke and cough. Andrea sends me a death stare, and I try my best to apologize.

"Sorry, I choked on my own saliva, like a moron." I manage to make my voice sound cheerful.

"Hi, Gabriel. Antonio back there says you have something for me?" Andrea smiles, and for a second, even I believe it's a sincere gesture.

"Good morning, Andrea and . . . I believe we haven't been introduced before," he says, looking at me with an intense stare that sends shivers down my legs. His hand's outstretched, waiting for me to shake it.

"No, I don't think so. I'm Avra." Fake flirting was my favorite thing to do on nights out. I'm a pro at it. He won't beat me at pretending. His hand is soft and too warm. Strong. His touch makes me want to puke all over the counter.

"Avra, beautiful name. Here, I see you are investigating Lola's disappearance?"

"Oh, you knew her?" I ask cheerfully in hopes it's not too much, too obvious.

"She was his mentee, tonta," Andrea answers, looking at me with the widest eyes, before he can say anything. "I'm sorry we brought you bad memories, Gabriel. We only knew about her job after we started our research. Actually, I was going to ask you about her."

"Yes, yes, she was a really bright young woman, very talented and promising. It was a pity, whatever happened to her. It was like the earth swallowed her whole. You know, deep down, I never lost faith, and I hope she's okay somewhere." Hearing that makes my cheeks turn hot, and my face is surely burning red now.

My rage boiling over doesn't escape Gabriel Cuervo. The look in his eyes changes, subtly, but enough.

Fuck. He knows.

His pursed lips draw the tiniest curve upwards, almost imperceptible. A sort of sad smirk shadows his face. I can't tell if he's delighted by the prospect of having to get rid of us or sad because he sincerely likes Andrea. It doesn't matter because we're *not* going to give him the chance. I'm glad. So he'll know it was us who got him, when the police cuff his ass.

"Well, there aren't really many leads to follow, so maybe I'll drop this one, you know? Not to ruin my reputation," Andrea chuckles.

"Pity, I thought you might be the one to finally put this mystery to an end. Antonio there told me this morning it would even be a special episode. He's going to be terribly disappointed."

While they talk, I examine his features. I can't blame Lola for falling for this guy, especially twenty-five years ago. He's an attractive man now, when he's just about to be retired. He must have been such a sight when he was in his forties. And with all that charm, it wouldn't be easy to tell it's completely fake, especially when a trusted relationship's already been established. The power dynamic between a mentor and a mentee... What chance did my tiny butterfly have against the experienced spider?

"Yeah, well, I'll see what I can do." Andrea smiles, taking the papers from him and nodding to me that we're leaving.

"We need to go to his place now," I murmur to her as soon as I'm sure he can't hear us.

"We can't leave now. We at least need to fake we're here for some reason," Andrea tries to reason with me.

"He knows. Staying here ten more minutes won't change that. It would only give him time to make a plan. We need to leave *now*. Trust me for once in your life, please?"

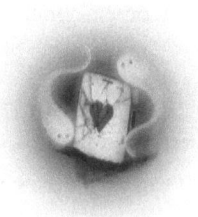

We drive as fast as we can without getting stopped and ticketed. It has to be done now. And fast. He must know we're up to something, and he's plotting what to do with us.

SPOOKY LOVERS

Gabriel Cuervo lives half an hour away from the library's city and the graveyard, in a very beautiful valley, down a dirt road, up a hill. He likes privacy and nature. It's a good thing he doesn't live near any small villages. We would've been spotted and stopped by a dozen elderly people by now and probably interrogated about where we're going and why. But the forest here protects us from unwanted stares, and we're far enough from the last house with enough crossroads between them and our car, so it's impossible to tell where we're heading.

We park and contemplate the house for a second. It's traditional: red walls, pink bougainvillea growing over it, a dark wooden corridor on the second floor, and a circular window in the attic. If I didn't know this was his house, it would look like a pretty home to live in.

"How come you always get me in trouble?" Andrea asks without even looking at me, her eyes glued to the red house, to the future, to what we're about to do.

"What are you talking about? This was *your* idea."

"Duh, once you put me in a situation where *this* is all I can do. Not helping out a bunch of missing women? Not me. And you knew it when you asked me."

"I didn't know there were more. I just wanted to help Ernestina find out who she was before that savage took her life . . . How could I have anticipated any of this? It's going to be okay, and I'll owe you one then. Happy?"

"Not in the slightest. You better be right," she replies, looking at me with smiley eyes and a serious face. "Vamos."

Andrea hands me a pair of white plastic gloves, takes an old credit card from her purse, and walks straight to the door, determined. She had to learn how to open closed doors when we were together because of my tendency to forget or lose my keys. She's mastered it. It only takes a bit of wiggling and pushing to get the door to Gabriel's secrets open.

"Ábrete sésamo." She winks at me. Despite being slightly mad and worried, she's also excited. I just want to get it over with as soon as possible and go back to

Ernestina's side. She must be worried sick right now. I send her a text via Spooky Lovers.

We're in, it's all good. Love you. It feels good to write it.

The house is spotless—so clean you could eat on the floor—and I doubt he's not going to notice we've been here. But if we manage to get enough evidence, we won't need to worry about it or him, anymore. He'll be in jail soon enough, rotting. And Ernestina and I will have our happy for now, and our happily ever after once I die.

"If you were a librarian serial killer, where would you hide your trophies?" Andrea asks, more to herself than to me.

"Well, I'd . . ." She raises her finger to shut me up. She needs to think, and my voice interferes. I close my mouth, turn around on my heels, and wander, waiting for her to have an epiphany.

"The basement?" Andrea muses. "No way, that would be too obvious . . ."

"Could we hurry up?"

"We could if you let me think," she replies.

If I were a serial killer, I wouldn't want to have my trophies on display, although I'd love to be able to, but what I would want for sure is to keep them close to me, as close as possible. In my office. Or better yet, my bedroom. When I finish my train of thought, Andrea's already reached the same conclusion. We look at each other and begin our search for the master bedroom.

Gabriel Cuervo's house is easy to explore. The kitchen and the living room are downstairs. Upstairs there's a library with dark wooden shelves and leather couches. There's also a tiny bathroom and a bedroom. This doesn't seem like the place he sleeps. It feels more like a guest room. There are only clothes hanging from the wardrobe and nothing under the bed or on the nightstand. You can see the valley from the corridor window.

"I was so sure . . ." Andrea complains, puzzled.

"It must be here; he wouldn't risk leaving those treasures anywhere else . . ."

We're beaten and decide to go back to the car and to the graveyard to tell Ernestina we failed. There's no plan C . . .

"Wait," Andrea whispers behind me.

I turn around and she's pointing up to the ceiling. Black lines on the wood outline a door up there. There's a tiny cord hanging from it. Andrea pulls it and a staircase unfolds between us.

"We got him," she says triumphantly. "This has to be it."

We go into the attic.

Right, here it is.

Gabriel Cuervo's *real* bedroom. The house, as his smile at the library, is just a façade, a cover so he can pretend to be a decent human being, hide the monster he really is behind the most common, boring home. But this room up here . . . this is where he can be himself. This is where the mask falls off, and the dragon comes out to play.

The attic's a big room with low ceilings and a circular window. It smells of wood, rain, and leather. There's a bed and bookshelves covering one of the walls. I figure these are the books he's not comfortable keeping in the library anyone can visit downstairs. There's framed art hanging from the walls, dark and romantic paintings of dead women emerging from the shadows.

Wait.

I get closer to one of them.

The fuckin' bastard.

That's Ernestina. She's lying with open eyes on a field so dark it looks black instead of green. The small daisies around her look more like stars in the night sky than flowers. Her expression is so peaceful. Her naked body broken, white against the grass. My heart beats, enraged. I turn to the other paintings. There's Irene, like Ophelia, drowned in a pond surrounded by water flowers, delicate as a lily herself. And Adela, against the gray rocks of a cold mountain.

He painted them. It wasn't enough to steal their lives, to violate their bodies. He turned them into his twisted muses, broken angels that would watch over his sleep.

"Help me here," I call to Andrea, who's looking under the bed. She looks at the painting, horrified. Tears come to her eyes as she looks around, and her gaze falls over the other two.

"Cabrón enfermo..."

Together, we take Ernestina's painting from the wall.

"Look behind," I tell her.

"There's nothing here."

"There must be, I'm completely sure," I say, feeling the back of the painting. Then my fingers find something. "There's something inside," I tell her.

Andrea takes her keys out and breaks the brown craft paper that protects the back of the frame.

There they are.

In each of the frames are plastic bags, as Ernestina told us.

I recognize immediately a piece of her starry dress. Her curls. The other two also have a lock of hair and a piece of cloth. Adela's uniform. Irene's jeans.

"I found something too," Andrea tells me, dragging a suitcase from under the bed. Inside, there are news clippings, missing persons posters, notebooks. Gabriel Cuervo really enjoyed knowing these women were still being missed, still cried upon.

"These are all probably covered in his prints," Andrea says.

"But those are not enough, are they? We also need to tell the cops where to find the bodies."

"Yeah, I've already thought about that." Andrea, with her gloved hand, takes out of her pocket a typed letter with the location of the three bodies. "I wrote it in a library away from home and printed it in another. We should be safe, and it should be enough. I've included a testimony saying that he confessed the crimes to us, which is technically true. They'll figure we're a priest or a lawyer or even a friend of Gabriel."

"He's going to spend the rest of his life behind bars. You're a genius."

My heart is so full of love, adrenaline pumping through my veins, I can't help it. I grab her face and kiss her. She's surprised, but her body's also full of energy and excitement.

Andrea kisses me back.

Her lips are like coming back home. Your first apartment. Your childhood houses. Places you used to call home but where you no longer belong.

Regret's already building up in my chest when the front door opens and closes with a thud. Andrea's eyes open wide. My heart jumps to my mouth, and my tongue dries.

"Oh, shit. He shouldn't be here. What the hell is he doing here?" I say before she presses her hand to my mouth so I don't make a sound. Boots walk on the wooden floor downstairs.

CHAPTER XI

AVRA

Andrea's hand presses tightly against my lips. She's trying hard to slow down her own breathing, but failing. I come back to my senses and remove her hand from my mouth. It's always been like this with us. We're a good team that way. I might be panicking, but the second I notice Andrea's out of her depth, I put myself together for her, as she's done so many times before for me.

The wardrobe where she's dragged me smells of vanilla and clean sheets. It's tiny, and the only light comes in from a small crack between the floor and the door. The whole house creaks with the weight of the librarian's shoes.

We used to laugh at stupid movie characters who hid inside the wardrobe where they were obviously going to be found. Turns out, when you're this scared, jumping out of a window's not the first thing that pops into your mind, and when you do think about it . . . that possibility has jumped before you had the chance to.

We'll laugh about this.

In a couple of days.

Okay, let's give it a couple of months.

"I know you are here, señoritas. And we all know you won't be leaving this house, don't we? At least not on your own two feet," he says from downstairs with the same charming voice he's used before in the library. "Why don't we try to make this a little bit more civilized? I'm not in the mood for a chase, to be honest. It's never been about the hunt for me."

His steps move to the staircase, toward his secret door. He's smart enough to have figured out we've already found his secret hiding place. Smart enough to know we're under the bed, in the wardrobe... somewhere still inside the house, clutching his trophies firmly.

"It's a pity, Andrea. I enjoyed our conversations, and your podcast; but don't you worry, I'm sure someone will follow in your footsteps and make a special episode about you."

Andrea's heart pumps against my ribs. How are we going to get out of here? It's two of us, we're younger, and we can beat the shit out of him. We have to try.

At least, we have to try.

"What a coincidence, don't you think? Lola starts haunting me after all these years, right before you two girls show up at my doorstep asking questions and going all Sherlock over my house... What, you did a Ouija board or something?"

My eyes relay all the thoughts crossing my mind to Andrea, but she doesn't like them. She's too afraid to fight. Paralyzed by fear, as people say. It's not just a common phrase; it's a very real thing. She can't even blink. Her wide eyes start to fill with tears. Everything she knows about what happened to Lola, to Irene, to Adela, to las Otras—it's all going through her head right now. Andrea is imagining Gabriel's hands on her neck. She's feeling all that pain already before he even gets to the last step of the staircase.

"We shouldn't have come," she whispers in my ear. "We shouldn't."

"Ernestina will help us," I grab her head and whisper back. I take my phone out. The blue light illuminates the wardrobe, and I try as hard as I can to keep a calming expression now that Andrea's going to see me clearly. "You'll see. She *will* stop him."

I write a text to Ernestina, but I'm about to hit send when the wardrobe doors open, and the librarian's huge hands yank me away from Andrea. He's stronger than I thought he'd be. His arms press me tightly. They cut off my breath. I grab my phone as firmly as I can. I need to hit that send button. Getting Ernestina inside of him is our only chance *out* of this house.

Our only chance *to survive* this day.

I press on my phone screen without looking and try to remember: What did my self-defense trainer always say? *Don't be picky*. Don't look for the right places to hit; just hit. Hit hard. The closest joint. With all your might, whatever strength you have left. It takes me a minute to react while Andrea and the wardrobe get farther and farther away. The librarian's fingers dig into my arms, making me realize we're nothing more than fragile, aching flesh.

"I'm saving you for last," he whispers in my ear once I'm in the middle of his room. That's all I need to come out of my fear trance. I kick his knee with my heel as hard as I can. He can't help it and liberates me. Reflexes are funny that way, not even Gabriel Cuervo can escape them. I put my phone in my back pocket and run toward the wardrobe and take Andrea by the hand, pulling her out and behind me.

He's waiting for us in front of the open door to the staircase, blocking the passage. We need to get past him if we want to leave.

"I'm curious to see what your plan is. It looks like your chances are not very good, don't you think?"

"Get out of our way," I say, and even I am surprised by the fact that my voice doesn't crack.

"Or else?" he chuckles, as if he were an unmovable mountain we won't be able to cross.

"There are two of us and only one of you. I'd say the odds are in our favor," Andrea says.

"I have two hands, and that's all I need," he says without moving. We need him to move from the door, closer to us, inside the room so we can attack him from two different angles. He knows it, and he's not going to give us the chance. We need to go *through* him.

I press Andrea's hand tight. She presses mine back.

We run toward him with all our might, as if we were charging against a wooden door, wishing we could tear down this one of flesh. We just have to make him fall—his feet are inches from the open staircase and a tumble that could incapacitate him.

He throws a punch as we approach and hits Andrea in the face. She falls to the ground, taking me with her, blood gushing from her nose. I crawl away from them to the bookshelves that cover the walls. He takes a step toward Andrea. She's the weakest now. I keep crawling to the shelves and grab a big fat book. He's too focused on Andrea, too sure he's got us to notice me getting to my feet. He wraps his hands around her ankle, tugging her closer to him.

"Gabriel," I cry, and he turns to look at me.

I slam the book down on his face. Gabriel stumbles and falls. He howls in pain, more animal than man. For the first time since we met, he sounds like the monster he really is.

"Come on," I say to Andrea. She stands up and kicks him in the ribs while he grunts, a mixture of anger and ache.

"This one's for Lola," she says, then spits in his face and holds my hand.

We throw ourselves down the small stairs, taking them two at a time, nearly falling over the last step.

The front door is open. Our car is right there.

Shit, we're going to make it.

I'm about to cross the threshold, out of the darkness into the light. A step between life and death, in the threshold of possibilities. My heart is pounding and my mouth is dry. My legs hurt, but I keep going. Andrea's hand slips from mine. I turn around without stopping, and her unhinged, terrified face moves away from me.

Gabriel's holding her by the waist, lifting her up. She's kicking the air. His nose is bleeding all over his beard and his shirt. He doesn't look like the civilized librarian of this morning but the monster within him. The dragon with his teeth sharp and ready, poisoned by bloodlust.

For a second, Andrea looks at me with pleading eyes. Her face is soaked in blood, too. Her expression changes abruptly. She's ready to fight.

"Run!" she howls.

My feet take root on the wooden floor while my arms just want to take flight. I can't leave Andrea with him. I hesitate.

Just a second.

Then, I run.

Don't stop.

Don't look back.

I keep running to our car.

I drive. Fast. Faster. To hell with the speed limit.

I drive away from Gabriel Cuervo.

Away from his hands, which I still feel on my belly, his fingers digging into my flesh, and all the lust in his voice murmuring in my ear.

"I'll save you for last."

Away.

From Andrea.

God, Andrea.

SPOOKY LOVERS

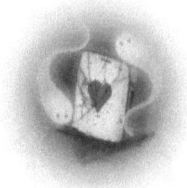

I stop the car at a curve in the road. Although I've surely been breathing all the way up here, I feel like I've held my breath the whole time, and now I need to catch up on all the air I've been missing. Rummaging through my pockets, I take my phone out and log on to Spooky Lovers, where my last text hangs unsent. *Mierda*. I press the little microphone on the corner of my months-long chat with Ernestina. My voice cracks the first time. I try again.

"Get inside of him. STOP HIM! He got her, Ernestina. YOU HAVE TO SAVE HER."

CHAPTER XII
ERNESTINA

A vra's frantic message sends me straight into panic mode.

I knew something would go wrong.

There's no time to reply; there's only time to act. I fly toward my burial site and into the darkness as fast as I can. I've gotten used to getting inside his head. The void engulfs me as soon as I focus on him. I've never concentrated so hard on anything in my death.

Come on, come on, bastard. Let me in.

From the void, I emerge behind his gray eyes once more.

We're inside his house. Andrea's screams pierce my ears and my heart. Not his. Her howling doesn't move him at all. If anything, Gabriel Cuervo hates loud noises, and he'll do anything to make her stop. It's not her pain that he craves, not what sets him off. It's never been. It's the opposite, actually. The stillness, the quietness of death, that's true ownership for him, the absolute lack of will inside a body. If he'd been able to, he would've kept us all. He's considering it right now. What if? Could he keep this one? Break her until her will is so destroyed she would resemble a corpse? Moving, talking, but dead inside.

Horrified as I am, that possibility would give me more time to figure out how to save her, and give Avra time to get the cops here as I'm sure she's doing now.

"You'll tear your throat apart before anyone hears you, ladronzuela, so better save it," he whispers in her ear, closing his hand around her neck even harder. Blood seeps into his mouth. They must have hit him when they were trying to escape. Andrea's face is also covered in blood. His nose hurts. He's never felt as humiliated as he does now. How dare they?

He quickly changed his mind about keeping her after the copper taste reached his tongue. It's nonsense. Impossible. Not with the other one on the loose. In fact, he doesn't have that much time before someone comes knocking on his door. He has to get rid of her and make himself presentable.

Following his command, in a second, while her teary eyes turn to him, Andrea's body relaxes, like she's given up. Her breath is ragged. But there's still fight left in her eyes, mingled with panic.

"Better," he says, allowing some air into her lungs. "You'll behave now, or it won't be pretty. We'll make it fast, you'll see. I appreciated our conversations; it's not my intention to make it hurt more than necessary. You're an intelligent woman. You understand you haven't left me any other choices here, right?"

Andrea nods.

Come on, come on, Ernestina. Think. What am I supposed to do? What should I do? This is not a memory. I'm here now, with them. I can save her. I *must* save her. Not just for Avra or Andrea herself, but also for me. I made him drink that glass of water; I can make him regret this. Turn himself in.

I concentrate. Problem is, there are no doubts, no regrets, no chances here as there were the night he killed me. There's nothing I can press on to. I have to create it from scratch. Compassion and mercy break out from me as if I were the Nile's fountains.

"Sit. We are awaiting company."

Gabriel guides Andrea toward his private library and pushes her onto a black leather couch while he cleans the blood on his face with a handkerchief. She's still crying but trying to comply. If I can see she's looking for a way to escape, something to hurt him with, then he can too. All my feelings, strong as they are, seem like not enough against the rage filling him right now.

There's just too much of it.

"Please, Andrea, don't try anything stupid," I murmur out loud, and all the lights inside his head are now pointing toward me. He turns, looks at one of the library's glass doors, and sees me.

I've fucked up.

"There you are, my sweet Lola. Good. This time I don't want you to go, not for a while. I've missed you. Knowing that you are here with me, deep inside me . . . Mmm . . . I was going to kill her and be done with it, but now I guess we could have some fun, the three of us."

Andrea stares in horror at the librarian talking to his own reflection in the mirror. Now she knows I'm here. At least she can be sure we're trying our best to help her. She must know Avra's on her way to the police station. We need a plan. But buying time's our better option. They're on their way.

We only need to buy time, Andrea.

Just a little time.

Only problem is, he knows it, too.

CHAPTER XIII

AVRA

I've never driven so fast in my life. I don't even know how I managed to follow my phone's GPS directions to the closest police station. I stormed inside, stumbling, babbling, in the midst of a panic attack. It was quiet and calm. They are only used to making IDs and such, maybe some petty thief or a battered woman who they'd dismiss as fast as possible. Not murder. Not life-or-death situations. Acting fast isn't in their blood.

"He's taken her. He's going to kill her. You must help her" is all I can get out. Eyes turn to me in disbelief, yet no one stands or comes to my aid. Small towns have many good things, but this is not one of them. I doubt they've ever seen a real emergency like the one we're in right now. They're more used to drunks causing trouble, and that's what the disbelief in their eyes shouts at me now.

I throw myself at one of the tables, pleading. Probably further reinforcing their idea that I'm just here to make a fuss. Intoxicated. Under some influence.

"HE'S GOING TO KILL HER! THE FUCK IS WRONG WITH YOU?"

There's no time for me to sit still and explain calmly.

"You need to calm down, young lady," says a voice at my back. "Come here, sit, and explain everything to me." One of the policewomen calls to me and offers a seat. "Have some water. Who do we need to help, and where is she?"

CHAPTER XIV

ERNESTINA

"I'll be with you in a minute," Gabriel Cuervo murmurs in Andrea's ear as he finishes tying her to his bed in the attic. Rags in her mouth won't let her scream for help as the doorbell rings.

From the attic window, Gabriel watches the cops arrive.

Inside his mind, I start screaming and stomping. Black needles and thread fly to me from the darkness of this empty space in his mind and sew my mouth shut. Black nails pierce my hands to his open eyes, so I have no choice but to look.

He's way stronger than I am.

I wait here motionless, powerless, broken, while he jokes around with the cops, offering them coffee or tea.

"I had to leave the library, you see? These nosebleeds are really bugging me . . ."

They talk about the ball this weekend and how excited everyone is. They apologize for disturbing him and leave.

They leave.

Gabriel Cuervo closes the door behind them and goes back upstairs.

CHAPTER XV
AVRA

I sit as patiently as I can at the police station, which is not very. I'm a mess. Who wouldn't be?

How long does it take to kill someone by strangling them?

Surely not as long as I've been sitting here waiting since I told them my story once, then again, and three times before they moved their asses to go check. The minutes tick by and I keep checking my phone, but nothing. My heart's about to explode. I can't think straight. I'm thirsty, yet every time I try to drink, I'm unable to.

I've bitten my nails to the beds. The policewoman holds my hand, trying to prevent me from doing it, from hurting myself. She doesn't know what to say; she knows as little as me. From her demeanor and expression, she's torn between believing me and going with the majority's opinion that I'm nothing more than a crazy one. They're so not used to this kind of situation that it's easier to label me as a troublemaker. I admit, a killer librarian in a small town in northern Spain doesn't seem likely, yet here we are. Also, it's their job to help us, isn't it?

I wish I could contact Ernestina, but she's not replying to any of my messages. I let her know the cops were on their way, but she hasn't even seen that, according to the app.

Did she help Andrea?

Oh, please. I had to run, or he'd have killed both of us, and we wouldn't have been able to get any help. Please, let her be okay.

Let her be okay.

"Let her be okay," I say aloud this time, only realizing it when I hear my own voice.

"She'll be fine," the policewoman reassures me as the station door opens. A bunch of cops enter, not as distressed as I'd have hoped, and Andrea's not with them. They pass us and enter the offices. Some of them shake their heads at me, as if they're annoyed.

"Wait here," she says and follows them inside. It only takes her a couple of minutes to come look for me. "Come, please."

I almost fall from my chair.

"You find her? Is Andrea okay? Did you get him?" I ask, before sitting down.

"You know that mobilizing police forces without good reason is an offense, right? You'll be lucky if you don't have to pay for all this nonsense out of your own pocket." The policeman's voice is so harsh it startles me. "We'll need to get you a drug test now, just to make sure."

"What? What . . . what is he saying?" I ask the woman, unable to believe my own ears.

"What *he* is saying is that your friend, Andrea, wasn't at Gabriel Cuervo's house, and she's never been there," he replies, even more mad now. "Against my better judgment, someone contacted her parents. She's apparently on a weekend holiday with a friend. Her girlfriend also testifies to this. We put those people under unnecessary distress for nothing. And about the house . . . All there was at that place was a well-respected member of our community, on sick leave, being disturbed by a prankster from what I could see."

"A prankster? What, am I supposed to have made all this up? Why would I do that? He's not on sick leave. He was at work this morning getting the fucking ball ready."

"Look, young lady, people like . . . you have been complaining about his decision of not having any of *your* books at the library, a decision the whole town backs, by the way, so I guess . . . this is all part of the campaign against him, so I'm not giving you any more of our attention. I'll let it pass this one time and won't get you tested; but I don't want to see you here again, and for your own good, I hope Gabriel doesn't come around here complaining about you."

"What the actual fuck?"

"Hey, lady, I'll have to ask you to mind your language. Don't make me regret letting you go."

"We're not activists, okay? Gabriel Cuervo is a dangerous man, and he has my friend, and he is going to kill her," I shout, until I notice the glances all around me.

"They checked." The policewoman intervenes, calming the waters. "There's no one else inside his house. No signs of her ever being there. No blood, nothing. She texted her partner to say she was going on a weekend trip to León with some friends, and she needed time to think and reconnect with herself. She's safe. She is not in his house. You can go now."

I could break these people's necks with my hands with the amount of anger I keep inside now.

"I hope you won't have to regret this and stay awake for the rest of your miserable nights," I say.

I get inside the car, tears choking me. I look in the rearview mirror.

CHAPTER XVI

AVRA

The graveyard gates are open. Ernestina's ravens fly frantically, cawing, rising up and falling, almost crashing to the ground, kamikazes of grief. Poison ivy grows over the gates, black flowers blooming everywhere. This display of all the signs of Ernestina's deep sorrow can't be good.

My ghost's right there, waiting for me but not daring to cross the gates to the other side. She's crying black tears that run over the bruises on her neck.

"Tell me she's okay," I demand in front of the gates, as if I, too, were obliged to stand only on my side of them.

"Avra I . . . I couldn't . . . I couldn't . . . He was so strong . . . I pushed as hard as I could. I pulled his tendons. I tried changing his mind, but I wasn't strong enough. He made me look. He made me look . . . I'm sorry. I'm so sorry . . ."

A storm breaks over us. Thick raindrops dampen my clothes and seep into my soul. I fall to my knees. My lungs close over themselves. Breathing is hard; the world spins. I feel like fainting, like dying. Ernestina fades behind my tears. My heart's broken into a million pieces. Or worse. It's imploded in on itself, keeping every last bit of suffering inside. Termites of guilt devour my stomach. I can't think straight. Andrea's face as she was pulled into the darkness by Gabriel Cuervo fills my mind. There's just agony. A void that will never be filled again.

We failed her.

Both of us.

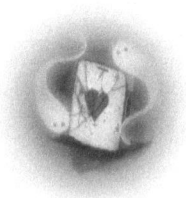

I wake up inside the church, covered by the soft blankets Ernestina bought for me. She's there, sitting on the remaining bench, just looking at me as if she had killed Andrea herself. My eyes are sore. The nails I bit down at the police station are itchy. My whole body hurts as if I had been beaten or run over.

"Morning. Or well, night, I guess," Ernestina's voice is soft but cold. Almost a whisper.

"Did you bring me here?"

"Yeah, the ravens helped. They're very strong, you see. You kept crying and then fainted . . . I thought you'd freeze if I left you at the gates."

"Thank you, Ghosty," I say, trying to condense in this one sentence that I don't blame her for what happened, that I still love her, that we need to stick together and fight back.

Her eyes, though, are cold as ice. "You're still in danger. Now that the cops showed up at his door . . . You need to move away, as far as you can. Just pack up whatever you need and leave. Don't you have family in the South?"

"What are you talking about? I'm not going anywhere. We need to stop him, now more than ever, as you say. Do you think I'm going to let the bastard who killed both of the women I love most in this world keep living his life as if it's nothing? As if your life and Andrea's meant nothing?" I protest, jumping off of the futon.

"What else are we going to do exactly? We tried, and it got her killed... And he *will* get you too if you stay here. I don't want to lose you. I'm begging you, just run away."

"I'm not going to leave you, and we'll figure something out..."

Ernestina floats in front of me. She's turning into a dark crimson shadow, the cold she radiates so strong now that it burns my skin. I have to take a step back. Her jasmine scent turns sour, coppery. She doesn't smell of her mother's perfume anymore, but of blood, mud, putrefaction, and decay. Her eyes are coals left in the fire. She looks twice her size. Maggots fall from her mouth, her ribcage breaks, and roots grow from it; flies surround her as a black cloud.

"I'm not asking. I'm ordering you to FUCKING LEAVE!" As she screams the last words, her ravens and the flies come at me like wild animals dying of hunger. I cover my face as the ravens pick at my hands and arms. The flies and bugs bite me, snakes crawl up my ankles. When I open my mouth to talk, flies fill it, and I choke on them.

I run from the woman I love.

Again.

I run until I cross the gates of the cemetery. The wild, angered cloud that follows me stops right there. In the distance, Ernestina howls.

CHAPTER XVII
AVRA

No one calls me to ask about Andrea.

I was half expecting it. Well, dreading it would be more accurate. They're probably pissed at me. Are they worried? Or are they sure I made it all up just to punish a librarian I've never heard of before? It seemed like a good idea at the time, saying she was going away for a couple of days, keeping her phone off so we'd have plenty of time to complete our plan. Now, that lie has kept her from being saved.

I'm relieved no one's tried talking to me because I wouldn't be brave enough to face her parents, or Eva. I'd break as soon as I heard their voices. I love her parents. They were always good to me. The thought of delivering the news of her murder to them breaks my heart all over again. They will come asking, of course. Soon. As soon as it becomes obvious she's not back home on Monday as she should have been, as she told them.

I'm driving home slowly. Tears blur my vision, and I'm too distracted to trust my reflexes. I keep looking at the rearview mirror. Her backpack still lies in the back seat.

The first thing I do when I get home is jump into the shower. I wish the warm water was enough to wash away this torrent of feelings. The taste of Andrea's lips assaults my mind. The regret of kissing her. Her eyes when she screamed for me to run. Ernestina's angry ghost and the way she bawled when I arrived at the gates. It's unimaginable what both of them went through while I was powerless, hopeless, waiting at a police station for a group of useless men to do . . . nothing. Nothing but pat Gabriel Cuervo's back. That thought, more than anything else, infuriates me and puts an abrupt end to my pity party under the shower.

I wrap myself in a towel and sit on my bed with Andrea's faux leather backpack.

"Come on, nena, you are a genius. Give me something," I murmur in case her ghost's already haunting me.

I deserve it, come on. Come torment me.

Her hoodie's in here. Her smell's still clinging to it. The definite power of death has not yet sunk in my heart nor in her belongings. Her phone's here too. It's off as we had planned, and I intend to keep it like that, at least until I solve this. I need to put an end to Gabriel Cuervo's murders. There's also her notebook. I used to laugh at her for her bullet-journaling hobby. I'm pretty disorganized, and my notebooks are all messy and ugly. Hers are cute, useful, and bright. Her whole life's condensed in these pages: podcast episodes, read books, even the amount of water she managed to gulp down every day . . . She loves plotting and hates surprises or being unprepared. I'm damn sure she had a plan C she hadn't shared yet. Andrea must've been saving it for the worst-case scenario in which we have fucked up every other option.

I'm still not ready to talk about Andrea in the past tense.

Pages and pages of doodles, appointments, and pictures. I cry over the pages as I go through the last year of her life. Then I stumble upon a scribbled note:

"Ernestina managed to make him drink a glass of water, but that was just a minor idea, easy to plant. He wouldn't be on the lookout for ghosts making him thirsty. But if all of a sudden he starts feeling remorse, or pity . . . He would know it's her, and it'd be easy for him to fight her off."

Oh, Andrea. So you knew . . .

When I took out my phone and said Ernestina would help us, right then and there, she knew we wouldn't be leaving his house.

Mierda . . . You should have told me. Fuck.

"From what I've seen, she would need to hide her presence better or else be much stronger, but we don't have time for training or anything like that. But what if . . . what if las Otras could help her? What if all the ghosts he created came for him at once? They must be where he dumped them, just as she is. Avra's been talking about ghosts all these years, and now, it all finally makes sense. I'll tell her one day. *She'd* love to hear it: You were right, pesada."

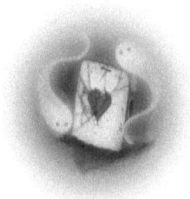

"What are you doing here? I told you to go and never come back!" Ernestina's turning back into the menacing ghost who tried to force me to leave—to leave *her*. To even move across the country. I speak as fast as possible in hopes my words catch her attention so she allows me to finish my reasoning.

"No, no, listen. I have a plan. It's not *my* plan; it's Andrea's. She wrote it all here." I shield myself behind the notebook in case there's another raven attack. "She'd already speculated that you wouldn't be strong enough to control him, to stop him if it came to it, before we went into his house. But what if we get the other ghosts to help you out? I'm certain this will work. I have that much faith in Andrea."

"Don't do this." Ernestina tries to get away, but she's softened.

It's working. I run toward her with the notebook up. I try to catch her, but my hand just goes through her as always.

"Come on, you know it would work. Hadn't you already thought about it?"

"Stop it!" she screams, crying; but she stops and looks at me with pleading, loving eyes.

"Ghosty, it wasn't your fault, and she's already given us the clues to end this. We must give it a try. For her. For you. For las Otras. And for those we can still save if we stop him."

Her ghost tears are like morning dew over a cloud of mist. She sighs, calms down, and talks.

"Okay, for those we would save. One last attempt."

CHAPTER XVII

ERNESTINA

After Avra told me the plan for the first time, we were both exhausted and needed to stop, even for a couple of hours, to comfort each other. We cried inside the church and lit candles for Andrea while I told Avra what happened after she'd left. I'm thankful to have been able to redact the experience this time.

We took turns, with one being vulnerable and the other strong. We fell for each other all over again. We merged as one, but this time it wasn't a sexual feeling, but something deeper, more meaningful. She breathed my pain in and exhaled forgiveness. I roamed through her mind, saw the kiss in the attic engraved inside her, but also felt the immediate remorse that took root in her stomach. Andrea's last words to her, to save her life . . .

I'm not made of stone. Of course it hurt me to witness that kiss, but . . . what does it matter now? Would it have meant anything if Andrea were still here? I doubt it. They'd have talked it out eventually, and when she was sure I wasn't going to freak out, Avra would've told me. It's one of the good things about being able to dissolve inside her mind: I don't need to rely on what I think she feels. I know it for a fact. So, I just did my best to cleanse her remorse while she allowed me in.

After tonight, we are renewed and ready to fight. But I need to be by her side this time. She can't do this alone, and I'm not staying here waiting for the news that she's dead to be delivered by the ravens or the bees.

"You said you've never tried getting out of the graveyard, so maybe, just maybe, you *can* do it. Maybe we can go to the burial sites of the other women, and I'm sure they'll help us," Avra explains while dressing in the middle of the church.

"Why are you so sure they're ghosts in the first place?" My voice sounds scared because I *am* scared. Way too many disappointments and failures in the last few days. Fear is the smart thing to feel.

"It makes sense. Their lives were cut short, like yours, and they're still missing . . . Killing him is the only way all of you are getting justice. Even if they don't remember, they'd have the same feelings you do. The same ache. The same longing. And if they remember . . . it'll be easier then." I also believe this to be true because Andrea believed it to be true. And we're not failing her again. I'd awaken their ghosts myself if need be.

I sigh and walk toward the church's door. It's now or an eternity of regrets.

"Okay . . . It might work . . ."

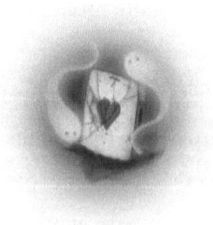

Avra stands on the other side of the graveyard gates. My heart would be racing if I had one. We are moving forward on speculation and hope alone, and it can go wrong at any minute.

"Come on, Ghosty, you got this." Her voice is as reassuring as she's capable of.

"If I vanish, or a black fire devours me . . . you have to promise me that you'll move south." I shake, floating closer to the gates.

"That's not going to be necessary. The bastard is going to pay." I'm sure her words serve the purpose of convincing herself as well.

"Promise me, or I won't move," I demand, really just to gain time and gather the strength to take this step . . .

"I promise," Avra replies, but I raise an eyebrow. That's not good enough. She adds, "I promise I'll move south with my family and never try to hunt Gabriel Cuervo again if anything happens to you as you cross the gates. Satisfied now?"

"Very much, thank you," I say, before closing my eyes and taking a deep sigh. I float gently toward the gates with eyes closed. It's a leap of faith for both of us.

I cross in the darkness.

And nothing happens.

"Ghosty, you did it. You're on the other side! You can open your eyes now," Avra informs me, convinced now that we'll succeed.

This time, we will get him.

CHAPTER XIX

AVRA

S potting a ghost underwater is not an easy task, especially if they don't know they *are* a ghost. The physics behind the fact that I was able to drive Ernestina with me to the lake is really way beyond what I can understand about this world. But here we are. She rides in the back seat, invisible apparently to any human being she doesn't want to be seen by.

"Oh, look, look!" she shouts, pointing out of the window.

"What? What's wrong?"

"I died in that cuuuurve," she says in a fake deep voice, before bursting into laughter.

"Ha. Ha. Great impersonation of la chica de la curva. Yeah, very funny."

"Shut up. It's part of the reason you love me." Ernestina winks at me in the rearview mirror.

"Enjoying the new situation, I see."

"Yes, it's like having a whole lot of new senses, you know?" she says with a curious voice. "I should've done this ages ago. This would have been so much fun."

In her notebook, Andrea followed the directions Ernestina had given us when she witnessed Irene's murder, and using her magic brain, she managed to identify the swamp where he dumped her. It's a very beautiful place.

"Not a bad place to rest," I say, contemplating the valley and the twilit sky.

"But a bad place to be dumped as trash," Ernestina corrects me.

I park, and we walk toward the water when the streetlamps turn on, casting an orange light on the darkling water. I look around, and the place is deserted. Not a soul in sight. He probably chose it because of that. What were the chances of getting caught? Close to zero?

"Have you considered that maybe she doesn't want us to see her?" Ernestina asks.

"No, it's not that. She's down there, I'm sure. Can't you feel her?" I reply, pointing to the black swamp.

"I . . . Yes. Actually, I can . . ." Ernestina smiles.

"Well, at least now we know for sure she's a ghost. Why isn't she coming out? Can you call her with your new special spooky senses?" I ask, worried about the success of our mission if the other ghosts we encounter turn out to be as stubborn as this one here.

Ernestina leans toward the water and dips her hand into the swamp. As expected, underwater, her arm turns into golden speckles that disappear in the depths, like underwater fireflies.

"Oh, no . . ." Ernestina stands and looks at me, rolling her eyes. "She's not coming out. She believes she's a mermaid."

"A mermaid. Really?"

"Yep, I'm afraid so. Can you blame her? I mean, I gave myself a fake name, and she's been underwater since the day he killed her. It's better to believe you're a daughter of the sea than a discarded, murdered woman, don't you think? She doesn't understand what she is or what's going on. She's been down there for too long, and just as I thought I couldn't leave the graveyard . . . She'll need a little push to leave the swamp."

I kneel on the shore, trying to make the most of the light reflecting on the water, but it's impossible to see anything, not even the glow of a mermaid-ghost.

"Can't you get in her head and communicate with her so she comes out here, so we can talk her into helping us?" I ask Ernestina.

"I'm trying, but . . . she refuses to listen. She pushes me out and screams. I think she's pretending it's a mermaid shriek, but . . . it's just a regular underwater, soundless scream." Her voice shows the pity and guilt she feels because this woman's here only because she looked like her. Ernestina's still not able to grasp the fact that *Gabriel Cuervo* is the sole culprit of any of this.

"So, what do we do then?" I wonder, standing again.

"You'll have to go pick her up." She's raised her brows.

"Me? Why me?"

"I'm a ghost," she shrugs.

"Exactly. Ghosts don't get wet, my love, nor drown. I hate having to point out the obvious."

"She wouldn't believe me; she knows my voice now and refuses to hear me out. Irene thinks I'm some kind of evil trying to lure her to her death . . . You must find the body and free it. She'd follow it out of the water."

I hate hearing *this* even more.

Overall, I hate that it makes sense.

"What am I now? An expert diver or what? I can't really hold my breath that long or see underwater. How am I supposed to find a decomposing body down there?"

"I can help with that, but you'll have to trust me. Take your phone out."

SPOOKY LOVERS

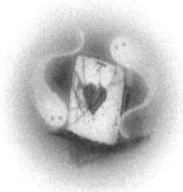

Apparently, there are people—lots, actually—into some really weird, kinky underwater shit on Spooky Lovers.

Ernestina plugs me in. The tingling in my toes and fingers produced by being online yet in the very real world at the same time makes me uneasy. My cyber-gothic, buffed-up vampire is wearing diving gear, state-of-the-art lighting equipment, and a pretty cool black-and-red diving suit that my ghost girlfriend has managed to... summon? She certainly didn't buy them with spectral money. If I had purchased this, it would have cost me a year's worth of podcast ads. I wonder if passersby would be able to see my supercool outfit, or would I just be a silly woman about to jump into the water in her jeans, because I certainly didn't change my real-world clothes, but it's not the time to ask Ernestina about it, we have bigger fishes to catch.

This is my life now, I guess, diving into a swamp in the middle of the night, searching for a corpse and its ghost who believes herself to be a mermaid, so she helps us fight the guy that killed my ex-girlfriend and my ghost girlfriend.

Never a dull moment since I installed this app. They should hire me to advertise their services.

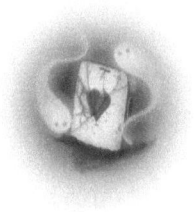

I jump into the water and swim the best I can. It's been ages since the last time I dove into the sea or a swimming pool. My only wish would have been that the app would also block the cold in my bones right now, but I figure that's too much to ask. I guess that also solves the question of the clothes. Yes, I'm probably just swimming in my jeans, and I'll have to drive back completely wet.

"Can you hear me?" Ernestina's voice resounds in my head as I go deeper into the darkness, out of the reach of the orange light of the streetlamps.

What the hell?

I try answering, but as I open my mouth, a big oxygen bubble comes out without carrying any sound.

"Oh, come on, just think the answer," she says cheerfully. This new seemingly almighty status of hers really amuses Ernestina, like a child with a new super-cool set of toys.

I can hear you, and it's quite disturbing, you know?

"Yes, I can imagine. But it's fun, isn't it? Turns out there are endless possibilities when you don't limit yourself to the norms imposed by the world of the living."

Yeah, right. I'm a bit busy here, amore. Is there a point to this, or are we just experimenting?

"Oh, no, yes, there's a point. I can guide you toward the body."

I follow her instructions, which is an arduous task considering the lack of references down here; there's just muddy water all around me, but teamwork makes the dream work, and the unmistakable glow of a ghost allows me to see Irene's body. Whatever is left of it.

Irene's ghost swims at the bottom of the swamp, followed by a school of fish. As I get closer, her light illuminates her corpse, tied to a wheel and a metallic toolbox. She's floating with her hair moving beautifully, and her jeans and sweater still on. She looks like an underwater flower ready to bloom. Her body has provided food for the fishes that form her court right now. Faithful creatures that belong to her as much as she belongs to them.

Irene notices my presence.

For a second, we stand motionless, facing each other. She's curious, like a deer spotted in the woods. Her eyes close. Damn, I know that look. It's the same one Ernestina gave me before turning into a succubus when she wanted me to leave.

Oh, no.

The school of fish around Irene dart at me as if she was an archer, and they were her thousand arrows. I cover my face with my arms. They hit me like tennis balls. It hurts like hell, but it could be worse, I guess. They're but tiny fishes after all. I need to keep moving forward, set her body free so she'll follow it out of the water. Crabs come to her aid, too, and they pinch my diving suit, weighing me down.

I swim toward the corpse, beaten and bitten by her fish and crabs, while she screams her soundless shrieks.

She's quite mad. You know, I could use some help here, Ghosty.

"Oh, yes, I see. Let me try something."

An underwater rain of tiny golden lights comes over us. Each lightning drop finds its way into the animals defending their queen. Ernestina controls them now, and they make way for me to work at cutting the rope. Irene's ghost floats around me, but without harming me. Her corpse aches for the night air, and as soon as I liberate it, it starts floating upwards. Holding tight to the rope, I swim toward Ernestina with Irene's body.

I pull Irene's remains carefully underwater. It'd make it easier for the cops to find the missing student now. No budget excuses for not searching the swamp. She'll be right here waiting for them on the shore. While I drag her body far from the water, Ernestina tries to capture Irene's ghost's attention. She's collapsed on the shore, gasping for air like she needs it. Like a fish out of water.

"Breath is all in your mind," Ernestina says. "Look at me and breathe."

Irene looks Ernestina in the eye and calms down. She looks at her legs as if she has never seen them, twists them, and separates them. There's a rectangle missing in her jeans. *Bastard.* Irene looks back at us, amused, then at her body, her corpse eaten by fish, destroyed by the swamp, the remains of the woman she once was. She takes her hands to her throat, clawing her nails at it like she's trying to dig up the words, staring at us, asking for permission to even try to speak, to raise her voice silenced for so long.

"Try. You'll see. You can do it." Ernestina nods at her with the most tender expression.

Irene makes some guttural noises, gasps, breathes, and finally talks. Her trembling voice is sweet and scared.

"Who am... What am I?"

"Your name is Irene, and you are a ghost."

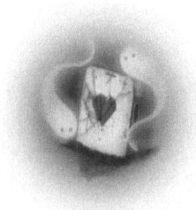

It didn't take as long as I thought to explain the whole situation to Irene. The longer you are dead, the deeper you fall into oblivion. Luckily for us, Ernestina was the most far gone, and Irene started remembering her life and her death as soon as we got to the car.

"My family... They must be devastated. My mother didn't want me to take on the scholarship. She said I was too young to be in a different country by myself... Oh, she's probably smothered my little sister with her worry now. I was supposed to clear the way for her, you know? I thought he liked me..."

Ernestina hugged her, and Irene had a meltdown in her arms, but got her composure back soon enough.

"Can you hug?" I ask, looking back at them in the back seat.

"Yeah... It feels like touching someone when I was alive. Why, can't you hug?" Irene responds.

"No, we can't," Ernestina sighs, looking at me in the mirror. "You could touch your fishes, and I can touch my ravens, but not the living, unfortunately."

"We have other ways . . ." I wink at her.

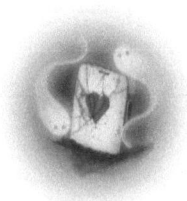

After a couple of false alarms, Adela's easier to find. Andrea had three different options for her burial site, and as it always happens, the third one was the charm. If she had asked my opinion, I could have told her this was going to be the one because out of the three, this was the only one with alleged ghost sightings. We followed her list because Ernestina thought it would be disrespectful not to do it, and that maybe Adela wasn't interested in haunting. Again, I was right, but I'm not going to brag about it. A single look is enough for Ernestina to roll her eyes at me and nod.

"Yeah, sweet Jesus, you were right, okay?"

When we cross through the big crystal doors, Adela's there in the middle of the office building hall, like Ernestina, minding her own business. She's invisible to the rest of the living rushing to the elevators or out of the doors. She's pushing daisies out of the concrete of the building, cracking the floors, and being followed by worms and snails, leaving wet trails behind them.

Adela remembers.

She was the last to go. Her body might be under a ton of concrete, but oblivion hasn't taken hold of her soul yet. She's still more from this world than the next. To our astonishment, she pushes a guy out of the way as he almost steps on her daisies. Not happy with that, she takes all his papers and scatters them around, laughing. The guy looks horrified. Adela, dressed in her supermarket uniform, lights up when she spots us, two ghosts and a living woman, staring at her in the middle of the day.

"I've been waiting for you. I knew you would come. I didn't know how many, but deep in my rotting bones, I knew there were more, and that there would be more unless we stopped him. There's another one now..."

Ernestina and I exchange remorseful looks.

"Yes, we tried to stop him and lost someone..." Ernestina tells her. "I'm sorry this happened to you."

Adela takes Ernestina's hands in hers. "You were his first. I looked a lot like you when I was younger."

Ernestina nods and breaks down in tears.

"Let's go outside," I murmur to the ghosts when I notice the security guard looking too interested in me, who admittedly looks suspicious just standing in the middle of the hall in front of a bunch of worms and snails.

Adela follows us out of the building. I stand back in the parking lot as the three of them hug each other. They merge into one another slowly, creating a big ball of black fire, forging them, hardening them like steel. The black flame is cold and devours all the light around it.

When they untwine their bodies, they all look different. Fearless. Fierce. This was it. This was what we were meant to do from the get-go. A team of badass ghosts ready to beat his ass and send him to the hell where he belongs.

I'm sorry, Andrea. It took us too long to figure it out.

"Let's end this," Ernestina tells me.

"Let's end him."

CHAPTER XX
AVRA

Fuckin' hell . . . I wish this knot in my chest would untie itself, or that it'd stop pushing me to do this. I'm a coward. It's been proven already, hasn't it? So why am I setting myself up for this? Why did I agree?

Love?

Yeah, right.

That.

I'm not afraid of dying. I never have been, even less so after meeting Ernestina and las Otras. Death is not the end, as I suspected. It's nothing but a change of habits . . . But I do fear pain. Physical suffering terrifies me. And I know that if this goes sideways, which is a pretty probable outcome, Gabriel Cuervo's going to hurt me. Maybe even more than he would have if we hadn't been snooping around. If we hadn't been a menace to his lifestyle.

Fuck. I hope this works.

The plan is simple. We're way past bringing Gabriel Cuervo to regular justice. We are on the "take justice into your own hands" phase. An arrest, a trial . . .

It's not enough anymore. He could have a great lawyer. They could dismiss our evidence coming from an anonymous source. It'd be easy for him to get away with it. Yet again. No. The plan now is way simpler than that. It's as plain as it should've been from day one.

The plan is to kill Gabriel Cuervo.

Yes, it's a bit of a broad stroke. Simple doesn't mean bulletproof, does it? But this might work.

It was actually Ernestina who first came up with the idea.

"The ball," she muttered suddenly, when we were brainstorming ways to finish the librarian's criminal career and his life—in a single blow if possible. "The anniversary ball. You said it's a masquerade to commemorate the one that took place twenty-five years ago, right?"

"Yes, they're using the same theme and everything. I believe it was his idea, a farewell gift for himself before he retires in a couple of years, a way to commemorate the night he . . . you . . ."

"My deathiversary."

"That night, yes . . ." Her sense of humor is completely back after meeting las Otras it seems. I'm glad. It was one of the first things I loved about her.

"Well, that's our chance there. He trapped me in that ball; we'll trap him in this one."

The only thing about the super-easy plan to kill Gabriel Cuervo that I'm not that comfortable with is that I will have the critical role of . . . bait.

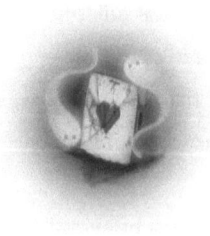

"How come you don't have any pretty dresses you can wear to this thing?" Ernestina asks me, looking at my wardrobe, puzzled.

"Because I don't usually wear dresses? Besides, I have a better outfit in mind," I reply, bewitched by the image of my love in my room for the first time. It's a sight I didn't think I'd ever enjoy.

"I'd love to see it. I need to give it my seal of approval." Ernestina smirks while I search. "I love your room. It's very . . . you."

My "very me" room consists of a queen bed, crimson walls, pictures of everyone I love, and book piles towering to the ceiling. I laugh. It could be very *us*.

"Now that we know you're not confined to the cemetery and that we'll get rid of the librarian . . . you could haunt my flat, you know?"

There's silence at my back. My heart sinks. Shit, did it come out wrong? Too soon, maybe? Why should she stay in the cemetery when she could be here with me? I don't dare turn around until I find what I'm looking for. I don't want to force her to reply.

"Here!" I say, holding out my expensive tuxedo, the one I've only worn at my best friend's wedding, forcing myself to sound excited and not at all freaking out because of her lack of an answer. We stay quiet for a second, looking at each other intensely. Is she as aware as I am that this might be our last night together?

"A tuxedo? Nice touch. Now, why don't you undress and try it on?"

That answers my unspoken question. And I go with it.

CHAPTER XXI

ERNESTINA

I've never seen anything more captivating than Avra wearing her purple tuxedo and a black lace masque. Adela's sparrows and my ravens helped bring some sparkling stones to add to it, and now she's wearing a piece of the universe on her face. Before we left her house, she took a small cameo from her nightstand, placed it around her neck, and tucked it under the black shirt.

"Andrea gave me this on the first anniversary of our friendship. I always thought it was weird that we were celebrating our last breakup that way, but she said we weren't honoring an end, but a beginning . . ."

One single tear peeked in her eye, but a smile replaced it soon enough. I didn't say anything. There was nothing for me to add.

"She'll protect me," Avra said. "Even if I didn't protect her, she won't leave me alone if I'm in harm's way."

It's almost showtime. Everything's ready. And despite how eager and excited I am to give Gabriel Cuervo his due . . . there's also a sadness creeping over me, a fog clouding my senses, my memory. I should be getting memories back from when I was alive. Instead, I'm losing bits of my life as a ghost . . .

Death's eating me up. I fear my time's coming to an end, one way or the other. I feel the light blooming over me, and the void. I'd rather choose which way it's going to be.

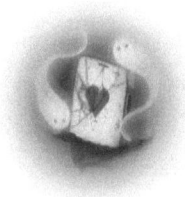

The library looks like a magical world. I don't see cardboard and glitter, cheap plastic decorations and tacky costumes. I see planets, constellations, stars, and creatures right out of a dream. As we gather around the doors, time folds, and I feel alive again. My night and this night are but one.

Avra has her masque on, and she mingles among the rest of the attendees while Irene, Adela, and I follow her invisibly through the people chatting and laughing. There's music playing. A string quartet. Everything about tonight's event has been carefully crafted to mirror that night twenty-five years ago.

Avra turns around, looking for something. For me?

"Ernestina," she murmurs very softly. I read her lips more than anything.

"What is it, my love?" I ask inside her head.

Don't freak out.

When she finishes saying it, the crowd in front of us dissolves, and I see it. Avra tried to warn me, but it's too late. Anger boils over in my chest.

There's my picture. A small altar-like pantomime next to the drinks and mini-sandwiches. I float toward it without noticing the presence looming next to it. There's even a candle lit here, some flowers, and a little notebook for people to write their memories of me and say how they miss me. And then I feel it.

Gabriel Cuervo's presence. He's leaning against the table with a smug expression on his face. He's enjoying the night. Wind rises inside the library. Lights flicker.

Please, Ghosty, stick to the plan. Not yet. Not here.

Avra's words soothe me. Yeah, the plan. It has to work this time, and improvising is not an option.

"Don't worry. I'll be good," I reply, so she can carry on with the plan without worrying about me turning the library into an unnecessary bloodbath. No matter how much he and everyone in this room deserves it. As far as I'm concerned, they're all just as guilty as he is. Every time they let him off the hook, they created a new chance for him to keep creating ghosts.

A couple approaches Gabriel Cuervo. A woman with a little girl walking beside her follows them.

Lola's family. *My* family. Something inside me should react. This vision should move me, bring forward some memories. Anything . . . but there's nothing. I know they were my family in my previous life, and Lola surely loved them more than anything in this world. But I'm not her. These people are nothing but strangers to me. Then I realize it's a blessing. I've been spared the pain of watching this little girl, Lola's niece, knowing I'll never get to know her, to hug her, to read her bedtime stories or hear her secrets when she's a teen.

It brings me peace, not to care about them at all.

They hug the librarian, sign the book, and chat with him as if he had been such a positive force, a beacon in my search . . .

"Enjoy your last hours on earth, Gabriel. Hell is waiting for you."

CHAPTER XXII
AVRA

The first bit of the plan is super easy. I just need to be seen by Gabriel Cuervo. The rest depends on how arrogant he is.

"Plenty arrogant" seems to be the consensus among Las Otras.

I stand here, motionless, in the middle of the library, people dancing all around me. I watch painfully as Lola's family talks with him, kisses him, hugs him. Apparently, they've kept in touch all these years. I can't imagine a bigger cruelty. He gorged on their pain while he painted Lola in his attic, while he touched the small piece of her dress . . . They write in the book, place some flowers on the small table, and leave. Lola's sister makes eye contact with me.

I shiver.

But I remain still until he sees me. An unmovable force in the middle of the library was going to catch his attention sooner or later. When I'm sure his eyes are locked on me, I remove my masque.

Gabriel Cuervo smiles, and I smirk back at him.

And now we waltz.

That's how I picture this interaction, following each other around the library, losing and finding one another in the sea of tulle and masques, moving to the rhythm of the music.

Purposefully, I let myself get cornered where he can trap me. His secret passage to his private cave I shouldn't know about. Because Lola didn't know about it while she was alive. And that's what he counts on. He moves carefully, leading my way, taking away all my options. He's already planned what's going to happen next. Ernestina saw the secret passage while inside his head, but she didn't know how to get in or, most importantly, out. But Irene does. Gabriel Cuervo showed it to her when he was courting her.

So here I am, in a corner of the library far from the partygoers' ears, with Gabriel Cuervo's shadow looming over me with hungry eyes, looking around for a way out, faking fear.

That part is *extremely* easy because I'm scared shitless already.

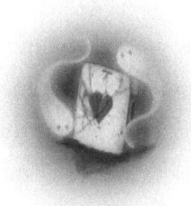

"He will think he's trapped you, but in reality, we will be there, waiting for him, to pay off all his debts with no one to help him out," Adela said when she laid out the plan.

And here we are, right where we wanted him. He comes closer to me, leans on me while fondling the shelf, looking for the book that will open the passage. I fall when the furniture behind me disappears. I crawl away from him.

"Why would you be so stupid to come here today? Is Lola with you already, or will she not show up until I have my hands around your neck? I'm starting to believe she enjoys the view," he says, closing the door behind him.

SPOOKY LOVERS

"Don't call her stupid," Ernestina says, making herself known in the dimly lit room. "And don't call me Lola."

CHAPTER XXII

ERNESTINA

Gabriel Cuervo's not scared. If anything, he looks amused when I show myself to him, here in his hidden realm. This is the first time I've been face-to-face with him since the day he killed me. I've only ever been inside him since I fell into his mind the night Avra screamed. My body's been eaten away by worms, flies, and rodents, and yet I can feel every inch of my flesh aching in his presence. His hands never left my neck. His lips never left my neck. His taste, my tongue. Fear never abandoned my heart. In his presence, my strength fails me. I'm weak.

Small.

I'm nothing.

But then I see Avra. And I remember. I matter. Not because she loves me, but because I love her. Because I'm someone capable of love still, after he took everything away from me. After he stole my last breath and my memory. My bright future. All the paths I could've taken. My successes and my failures. All the heartbreaks. All my first kisses.

"This must be every librarian's dream," he mutters. "The ones who love *Wuthering Heights* anyway," he laughs.

If arrogance was the key for this plan to work, we're doing great.

"What's your plan here, exactly? Because this hasn't worked out once already."

Adela and Irene become visible for him, and then fear crosses his eyes for a second. We all hold hands in front of him. One ghost he could stomach. It was part of his fantasy, after all. But three of us, we might have a chance, eh?

"Surprise," Avra says, leaning against the wall with folded arms. "This is going to go a bit more *Amontillado* style. I'm glad you love ghost stories so much; you're about to become one."

We take the chance while it lasts, and the three of us jump inside him, ready to hijack his mind.

CHAPTER XXIV

AVRA

It's not working as well as we hoped, or as Andrea had hoped when she wrote the notes that inspired "The Simple Plan" that's going sour rapidly.

Possessed as he is by not one but three ghosts, Gabriel Cuervo still manages to walk menacingly toward me, laughing. If las Otras have managed to do anything in there, it's certainly been to make him look like a psychopath for the first time since I met him.

At least, if he kills me now, I'm wearing a killer ghost outfit.

"Girls, I don't know what's going on in there, but you better hurry," I murmur, as I realize my back's now against the wall and the only way out would be through the door, into the ball. But then the plan would've failed for sure. Staying here is our one and only, our last, shot.

No one will help me if I go outside now, crying that he attacked me. Not after the incident with the useless police force of this damned town. Not with everyone so in love with him.

SPOOKY LOVERS

Gabriel Cuervo's hands close around my neck. Looking into his eyes, I see them all. The three of them. My ghost and las Otras, fighting like Amazons to kill him from the inside.

He doesn't talk to me. He only grunts. I can't breathe. I scratch his hands and his face with my nails, but I've bitten them down, so I'm not hurting him as much as I would love to. At times, his pressure softens, but those brief moments of relief are worse because they give me hope.

And hope is the true horror here.

Bright lights fill my eyes, blur my vision. Andrea's cameo burns over my skin as if it had been placed over a fire. He's lifting me up from the floor. This is it. There's a glow behind him. Am I hallucinating before my heart stops?

"Andrea," I pray, although I'm sure no sound comes out of my mouth.

It can't be, but it is. There she is, my bright Andrea, my savior. I knew she would haunt my ass for getting her killed.

"Andrea . . ." I say again to make sure I'm still here.

Andrea's ghost winks at me, grabs his head with both hands, and doesn't hesitate. His hands let go of me, and I fall to the ground.

I hear the snap of bones. A thud. Gabriel's dead face falls next to mine.

And I faint.

CHAPTER XXV
ERNESTINA

G abriel Cuervo's dead.

His body is rotting inside the library's secret office. It won't be long until they find his corpse. When the smell inside the building becomes insufferable. When the search for him everywhere else fails.

We tried to stop his heart from the inside. It beat in my hands as I pressed it. And the hands of las Otras joined mine. We pressed, and it wasn't enough, and we almost got Avra killed. She swears Andrea showed up and snapped his neck.

"She's the newest one," Adela said. "She still has one foot in this realm, so she could have done it. She could be strong enough."

But I didn't feel her presence, nor did las Otras. My theory remains that someone knew about the passage, walked in on him strangling Avra, and decided to put an end to it. Panicked and left before she could come back to it. Or before we left his cold body. Maybe he wasn't keeping all his secrets to himself. Maybe he was sharing.

Whatever the case, it was exactly the end he deserved. He wasn't going to feel ashamed if he had been caught and put on trial. He was a coward, and he would've ended his own life in prison if he knew he would be found guilty. And there was always the chance that he would get away with it.

This way, we took justice into our own hands. And you know what? It feels right. It feels so good to know he's gone for good that I almost cry from happiness.

I don't give a damn if it's not right to admit it. I'm tired of being the lonely ghost, the victim without a name. I'd rather be the blade of revenge. I could not save Andrea. I wish I had been the one to save my love, but I'm grateful to whoever did it—Andrea or not. There's not a single drop of regret in me.

I can't feel his spirit around, so I guess he didn't have any unfinished business, but lots of debts to pay in hell. I don't think there's such thing as a heaven, to be honest. I know it's difficult to imagine one without the other, but I truly believe that I can feel it already, that the light is just the chance to rest, to feel nothing, to be completely free. But some people are so awful, and create such an amount of pain, that they have to cleanse their souls before they rest.

Cleanse by fire.

Until the pain they have caused ceases to exist, until the last person to ever shed a tear because of them is at rest. Maybe when the last person to ever cry over las Otras or me dies, he will rest. But not a single second before. I hope he suffers all the way through it, all the pain he caused multiplied a thousand times.

When Avra woke up, the ball was already over, and Gabriel's body was cold. He peed himself and lay there, in a puddle, with his eyes open. Irene showed Avra how to get out, and we drove to her place. She's sleeping. There are black fingerprints forming on her neck already. It's going to hurt for a bit.

Adela and Irene have left. They're going to haunt their families for a bit, bring them some peace if they can. Meanwhile, I look at Avra sleeping in her bed. It's been a wild ride since we met on Spooky Lovers, but it's coming to an end. I realize now that the light, the numbness, the freedom from this world and its suffering, it was always there. My own rage was keeping me here, blind to it. Now . . . Having met Adela and Irene, I see how my mind is dissolving in time. How I stopped being Lola and how, soon, I won't be Ernestina either, but one of those mindless ghouls that Avra was hunting.

Sudden sadness overcomes me when I admit to myself that this is never going to be my home. There's no way this will work. We've lied to ourselves. In the room, there's a wall covered with pictures. One particular picture catches my attention. Not only because I've never seen Avra look as happy as she does there, but also because Andrea's in it, too. They're hugging. And laughing. It must've been someone's wedding because they're both wearing fancy suits and makeup. They did look good together.

I cry.

For Andrea.

For Avra.

For myself.

Avra's fingers brush my tears away.

She's awake.

"We need to talk," I say, immediately regretting that I've started our goodbyes with a cliché.

CHAPTER XXVI

AVRA

Tonight has been the longest night of the year, yet it's felt like the shortest of my entire life. I kept praying for the sun to implode, to cease to exist, so the night would last forever. Forever protected from its light, I'd never have to say goodbye to Ernestina.

I respect her decision, don't get me wrong. How could I not? But it breaks my heart nonetheless. By the look in her eyes, it breaks hers too. We need to go, but I don't want to go.

"Five more minutes," I whisper as she moves toward the door.

"Avra . . ." She turns back to me. "It's time. We'll always crave five more minutes, then five more . . . and we'll never be able to do it. We need to. I need this, my love. I'm disappearing. Do you want to see me turn into a mindless ghost? A presence without a mind of my own? Now that he's gone, I can tell the process is speeding up."

"I know," I sigh. "I know."

I draw my hand forward and *into* her cheek, letting her electricity infect me.

"Okay, let's go," I say, getting my backpack ready.

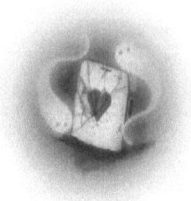

We go back to the graveyard.

I've promised Ernestina I'll deliver the evidence we have to the policewoman who wanted to help me, so she will be found, and her family, Lola's family, can finally rest. And Andrea's, Adela's, and Irene's.

Done deal. He's disappeared. It makes sense that they would search his house. The amount of stuff he had in his attic is going to be as good as a confession. I hope they don't find his body until the rats have eaten his face off.

Ernestina didn't want to visit Lola's family as las Otras had.

"It's not my family anymore. I'm not Lola. It'd be wrong because I have nothing to offer them . . ."

I respect that. I'm glad we have the chance to say goodbye to each other. Just the two of us. Just as we started. In the graveyard, two women, nervous and in love.

"Come with me," she says, finally getting out of the car without touching the doors.

Once we cross the gates, the whole place lights up like a Christmas tree. The ravens fly above us, cawing a sad song, marigolds sprout all around, fireflies surround us, and all those other fearful nocturnal creatures come to meet us.

Ernestina's eyes are full of tears and love. She looks at me, and I understand.

It's our farewell party.

SPOOKY LOVERS

"We needed a proper goodbye," she whispers in my ear. "My heart is yours. We'll see each other again. Trust me. This is just a . . . see you later. Just try not to leave unfinished business, and don't turn into a ghost. Please make me wait."

"I'll try my best," I laugh, full of sadness. My voice cracks, even though I've promised myself I wouldn't make this more difficult for her. I can't keep my own promise to myself.

Ernestina takes a step back, smiling at me. The most tender smile I've ever seen. Eyes full of peace. "I love you, Ghost Hunter."

"I love you, Ghosty . . ."

Tonight, I say goodbye to the matching Victorian dresses and our adopted cats wearing our wedding rings on little cushions. I'm saying goodbye to the kids we will never have. They were going to be so cute.

So cute.

Tonight, I say goodbye to the love of my life.

And we will have one hell of a goodbye party.

EPILOGUE

AVRA

I kept my promise to Ernestina, obviously. Although the policewoman had a bit of a hard time putting two and two together, as soon as rotting Gabriel Cuervo was discovered, the pieces fell into place on their own. Andrea's body was the first to be recovered. She was in his backyard. We left Irene on the shore, so she was easy. Lola's family were on every morning show, grateful to the anonymous source that had offered the location of their loved one's remains. They haven't found Adela yet.

I didn't attend Andrea's funeral. Her family made it abundantly clear that I wasn't welcome there. Eva shouted it out very eloquently on the phone in case I had any doubts. I don't blame them. I'm also terribly mad at me. I'd also consider being mad at the cops that didn't listen to me when I first asked them for help, when saving her was still a possibility, but what do I know? I am the one who put her in harm's way in their eyes.

I might not blame them, but I'm not happy about it either. I wish I was more resilient, but . . . I am who I am. I'm a person who blames killers, *and only killers*, for their actions.

And I lost her, too. But I get it. Seriously.

So I waited until everyone was gone to visit her tomb. I saw the service at a distance. No one spotted me. It was very nice. All our friends were there, her family, too. The cemetery was packed with love, and she would've loved it.

I had hopes, obviously, that she would appear right next to me, to tell me that now I owe her two. But she didn't show up. I guess the light is the real definitive part of being dead, and once she killed Gabriel Cuervo, there was nothing else for her to do. She was one to never leave anything to tomorrow. Unfinished business wasn't her thing at all. I would argue she still had tons of it with her, but I'd lose that battle. When I finally went to her tombstone, there was nothing more than cold stone and sadness. I kissed the stone and left.

I moved south the month after everything went down. It's too hot during the summer and too cold during the winter, but I have family here. They offered me a job in their shop, and I soon found a place where I could keep recording my podcast, to maintain some sort of normality in my life. I've changed it, though. It's not about cemeteries and ghosts anymore, but about unsolved crimes and missing persons. I'm not yet as good as Andrea was, but at least I feel closer to her. Like I'm helping others. As Ernestina told me to. I couldn't bear having to lose them both. All the memories. I visited the graveyard every day during that month, and it was not healthy. I couldn't eat or sleep. The hope that they'd come back was eating me alive. It was just not good for me. And none of them would've wanted that.

I'm happy here. Well, sort of. Time will heal these wounds, I hope. That's what my therapist says. She doesn't know about the ghost part, only the loss, the trauma. I close the shop and walk home alone. It's warm and the streets are full of life. People are having fun, enjoying spring after the dark winter. I sit on my favorite terrace and order a beer. The waiters know me already. They're friendly, like having friends but not needing to commit. I'm not ready for that yet.

My phone starts chiming. Weird. That's not how it sounds now. I've never set "The Man Who Sold the World" as my notification sound. There's a Spooky Lovers notification, although I deleted the app months ago. That can't be. I've even changed my smartphone.

I open the message.

A winking emoji.

www.ingramcontent.com/pod-product-compliance
Lightning Source LLC
LaVergne TN
LVHW011047100526
838202LV00078B/3752